THE MAKER
OF GARGOYLES
And Other Stories

THE MAKER OF GARGOYLES
And Other Stories

CLARK ASHTON SMITH

INTRODUCTION BY
DARRELL SCHWEITZER

WILDSIDE PRESS

THE MAKER OF GARGOYLES AND OTHER STORIES

For more information, contact:

Wildside Press
P.O. Box 301
Holicong, PA 18928-0301
www.wildsidepress.com

CONTENTS

KLARKASH-TON, SORCERER-POET

lark Ashton Smith was a prodigy, who wrote Arabian Nights novels in his mid-teens and was heralded as a major voice in American poetry by the time he was nineteen. In one frantic burst in the middle 1930s, he wrote nearly a hundred strange, wondrous, and grotesque stories, most of which were published in *Weird Tales, Strange Tales, Wonder Stories,* and other pulps, but he was by no means a conventional pulp writer. A direct heir to Edgar Allan Poe and to the late Romantics and Decadents, a translator of Baudelaire, Smith wrote in baroque, jeweled prose of distant times and remote planets, of baleful magics and reanimated corpses, lost lovers, eldritch gods, and inexorable fate. He is also a writer whose works refuse to die, even after nearly a century.

Think of him as the sorcerer-poet, alone in his eyrie in the dry California hills, dreaming his strange dreams and creating his unique worlds – of Zothique, the Earth's haunted last continent at the end of time, Hyperborea, a prehistoric land, Poseidonis, the last foundering isle of Atlantis, and Averoigne, an unhistoried province of medieval France, thick with vampires. Think of the visions his stories conjure up as *sendings*, written in strange runes, transported from the sorcerer's lair by indescribable genii or winged spirits. His stories are altogether unlike anyone else's and quite wonderful, among the treasures of fantastic literature.

But we must not make Smith himself into a fantastic creation. He was a Californian, born in 1893, thus three years younger than H.P. Lovecraft. His schooling ended early, but he educated himself, it is reported, not only by poring over every book he could find, but by reading the dictionary cover to cover. He lived most of his life in a remote cabin, in semi-poverty, doing occasional outdoor, odd jobs to meet his modest expenses. He despised the confines of an office or shop. When he needed money, he preferred to pick fruit or dig wells.

He always thought of himself primarily as a poet, and worked steadily on poetry from his youth to old age. His first book, *The Star-Treader* (1912) was a volume of gorgeous, cosmic poetry somewhat in the manner of, but superseding the work of his then-famous mentor, George Sterling, who, along with Ambrose Bierce, was one of the leading figures in the California literary scene. Most of Smith's fiction was written when he needed money as his parents entered their dotage. While some of the science fiction he wrote for Hugo Gernsback he candidly described as hackwork in his *Selected Letters*, the effort awakened new potential in him. His poetry is still admired, but it has been sidelined by the post-Pound, post-Eliot developments of the middle 20th century which seems to eschew both elegance and coherence; therefore it is his fiction which has become the basis of his permanent, popular reputation.

In many ways he was anything but the reclusive aesthete. His letters show him to have been quite practical-minded, willing to try new markets, attempting to reach out (albeit not always successfully) to markets as diverse as *Astounding Stories, Terror Tales,* and *Esquire.* In the early 1950s we find him suggesting to his then-agent Forrest J. Ackerman that some of his older, frequently erotic stories, if shorn of a bit of their more ornate prose, might be submitted to the new magazine, *Playboy.* Meanwhile Smith did what he could to develop his skills in painting and sculpture, at one point making more money selling weird little statuettes, mostly grotesque heads and faces, and alleged portraits of sinister cosmic entities.

He was a friend and correspondent of H.P. Lovecraft. Although the two never met, they came to esteem one another highly. At first, Lovecraft wrote a admiring letter to Mr. Smith, the Poet, but soon the relationship warmed up. They became colleagues, Lovecraft inspiring Smith as much as Smith inspired Lovecraft. Elements of Lovecraft's Cthulhu Mythos began to appear in Smith's stories, as did various ancient gods and forbidden tomes of Smith's invention in Lovecraft's work. Lovecraft's classic "The Whisperer in Darkness" even contains a playful reference to "The Commorium Myth Cycle" – of which "The Testament of Athammaus"in the present volume is a part – of "the Atlantean priest, Klarkash-Ton."

Together, Lovecraft and Smith, with a third colleague, Robert E. Howard, dominated *Weird Tales* in the 1930s and significantly shaped fantastic literature for decades to come. While Smith's output diminished after about 1940, he continued to write into the late '50s, during which time his work reached as larger audience as August Derleth's Arkham House publishing company issued more and more Smith in book form. Altogether, his fiction took up six volumes. *Selected Poems* appeared in 1971. His *Selected Letters* has appeared recently. He married late in life, moved away from his cabin, and died in 1961.

But in books like the present one, he is not dead. He may never be as popular as J.R.R. Tolkien or T.H. White or J.K. Rowling, but by the connoisseur of the darkest of dark and ironic fantasy, Smith will always be read. His work lives. Here is some of it. This book is a good place to start, if you've never read him before.

Read this. It will change you forever.

Darrell Schweitzer
02 June 2004

THE ABOMINATIONS OF YONDO

The sand of the desert of Yondo is not as the sand of other deserts; for Yondo lies nearest of all to the world's rim; and strange winds, blowing from a pit no astronomer may hope to fathom, have sown its ruinous fields with the gray dust of corroding planets, the black ashes of extinguished suns. The dark, orblike mountains which rise from its wrinkled and pitted plain are not all its own, for some are fallen asteroids half-buried in that abysmal sand. Things have crept in from nether space, whose incursion is forbid by the gods of all proper and well-ordered lands; but there are no such gods in Yondo, where live the hoary genii of stars abolished, and decrepit demons left homeless by the destruction of antiquated hells.

It was noon of a vernal day when I came forth from that interminable cactus-forest in which the Inquisitors of Ong had left me, and saw at my feet the gray beginnings of Yondo. I repeat, it was noon of a vernal day; but in that fantastic wood I had found no token or memory of a spring; and the swollen, fulvous, dying and half-rotten growths through which I had pushed my way, were like no other cacti, but bore shapes of abomination scarcely to be described. The very air was heavy with stagnant odours of decay; and leprous lichens mottled the black soil and russet vegetation with increasing frequency. Pale-green vipers lifted their heads from prostrate cactus-boles and watched me with eyes of bright ochre that had no lids or pupils. These things had disquieted me for hours past; and I did not like the monstrous fungi, with hueless stems and nodding heads of poisonous mauve, which grew from the sodden lips of fetid tarns;

10

and the sinister ripples spreading and fading on the yellow water at my approach were not reassuring to one whose nerves were still taut from unmentionable tortures. Then, when even the blotched and sickly cacti became more sparse and stunted, and rills of ashen sand crept in among them, I began to suspect how great was the hatred my heresy had aroused in the priests of Ong; and to guess the ultimate malignancy of their vengeance.

I will not detail the indiscretions which had led me, a careless stranger from far-off lands, into the power of those dreadful magicians and mysteriarchs who serve the lion-headed Ong. These indiscretions, and the particulars of my arrest, are painful to remember; and least of all do I like to remember the racks of dragon-gut strewn with powdered adamant, on which men are stretched naked; or that unlit room with six-inch windows near the sill, where bloated corpse worms crawled in by hundreds from a neighboring catacomb. Sufficient to say that, after expending the resources of their frightful fantasy, my inquisitors had borne me blindfolded on camel-back for incomputable hours, to leave me at morning twilight in that sinister forest. I was free, they told me, to go whither I would; and in token of the clemency of Ong, they gave me a loaf of coarse bread and a leathern bottle of rank water by way of provision. It was at noon of the same day that I came to the desert of Yondo.

So far, I had not thought of turning back, for all the horror of those rotting cacti, or the evil things that dwelt among them. Now, I paused, knowing the abominable legend of the land to which I had come; for Yondo is a place where few have ventured wittingly and of their own accord. Fewer still have returned — babbling of unknown horrors and strange treasure; and the lifelong palsy which shakes their withered limbs, together with the mad gleam in their starting eyes beneath whitened brows and lashes, is not an incentive for others to follow. So it was that I hesitated on the verge of those ashen sands, and felt the tremor of a new fear in my wrenched vitals. It was dreadful to go on, and dreadful to go back, for I felt sure that the priests had made provision against the latter contingency. So after a little I went forward, sinking at each step in loathly softness, and followed by certain long-legged insects that I had met among the cacti. These insects were the color of a week-old corpse and were as large as tarantulas; but when I turned and trod upon the foremost, a mephitic stench arose that was more nauseous even than their color. So, for the nonce, I ignored them as much as possible.

Indeed, such things were minor horrors in my predicament. Before me, under a huge sun of sickly scarlet, Yondo reached interminable as the land of a hashish-dream against the black heavens. Far-off, on the utmost rim, were those orblike mountains of which I have told; but in between were awful blanks of gray desolation, and low, treeless hills like the backs of half-buried monsters. Struggling on, I saw great pits where meteors had sunk from sight; and divers-colored jewels that I could not name glared or glistened from the dust. There were fallen cypresses that rotted by crumbling mausoleums, on whose lichen blotted marble fat chameleons crept with royal pearls in their mouths. Hidden by the low ridges, were cities of which no stela remained unbroken — immense and immemorial cities lapsing shard by shard, atom by atom, to feed infinities of desolation. I dragged my torture-weakened limbs over vast rubbish-heaps that had once been mighty temples; and fallen gods frowned in rotting psammite or leered in riven porphyry at my feet. Over all was an evil silence, broken only by the satanic laughter of hyenas, and the rustling of adders in thickets of dead thorn or antique gardens given to the perishing nettle and fumitory.

Topping one of the many moundlike ridges, I saw the waters of a weird lake, unfathomably dark and green as malachite, and set with bars of profulgent salt. These waters lay far beneath me in a cuplike hollow; but almost at my feet on the wave-worn slopes were heaps of that ancient salt; and I knew that the lake was only the bitter and ebbing dregs of some former sea. Climbing down, I came to the dark waters, and began to lave my hands; but there was a sharp and corrosive sting in that immemorial brine, and I desisted quickly, preferring the desert dust that had wrapped me about like a slow shroud.

Here I decided to rest for a little; and hunger forced me to consume part of the meager and mocking fare with which I had been provided by the priests. It was my intention to push on if my strength would allow and reach the lands that lie to the north of Yondo. Theses lands are desolate, indeed, but their desolation is of a more usual order than that of Yondo; and certain tribes of nomads have been known to visit them occasionally. If fortune favored me, I might fall in with one of these tribes.

The scant fare revived me, and, for the first time in weeks of which I had lost all reckoning, I heard the whisper of a faint hope. The corpse-colored insects had long since ceased to follow me; and so far despite the eeriness of the sepulchral silence and the mounded dust of timeless ruin, I had met nothing half so horrible as those insects. I began to think that the terrors of Yondo were somewhat exaggerated.

It was then that I heard a diabolic chuckle on the hillside above me. The sound began with a sharp abruptness that startled me beyond all reason, and continued endlessly, never varying its single note, like the mirth of an idiotic demon. I turned, and saw the mouth of a dark cave fanged with green stalactites, which I had not perceived before. The sound appeared to come from within this cave.

With a fearful intentness I stared at the black opening. The chuckle grew louder, but for awhile I could see nothing. At last I caught a whitish glimmer in the darkness; then, with all the rapidity of nightmare, a monstrous Thing emerged. It had a pale, hairless, egg-shaped body, large as that of a gravid she-goat; and this body was mounted on nine long wavering legs with many flanges, like the legs of some enormous spider. The creature ran past me to the water's edge; and I saw that there were no eyes in its oddly sloping face; but two knifelike ears rose high above its head, and a thin, wrinkled snout hung down across its mouth, whose flabby lips, parted in that eternal chuckle, revealed rows of bats' teeth.

It drank avidly of the bitter lake; then, with thirst satisfied, it turned and seemed to sense my presence, for the wrinkled snout rose and pointed toward me, sniffing audibly. Whether the creature would have fled, or whether it meant to attack me, I do not know; for I could bear the sight no longer but ran with trembling limbs amid the massive boulders and great bars of salt along the lakeshore.

Utterly breathless, I stopped at last, and saw that I was not pursued. I sat down, still trembling, in the shadow of a boulder. But I was to find little respite, for now began the second of those bizarre adventures which forced me to believe all the mad legends I had heard.

More startling even than that diabolic chuckle was the scream that rose at my very elbow, from the salt-compounded sand — the scream of a woman possessed by some atrocious agony, or helpless in the grip of devils. Turning, I beheld a veritable Venus, naked in a white perfection that could fear no scrutiny, but immersed to her navel in the sand. Her terror-widened eyes implored me and her lotus hands reached out with beseeching gesture. I sprang to her side — and touched a marble statue, whose carven lids were drooped in some enigmatic dream of dead cycles, and whose hands were buried with the lost loveliness of hips and thighs. Again I fled, shaken with a new fear; and again I heard the scream of a woman's agony. But this time I did not turn to see the imploring eyes and hands.

Up the long slope to the north of that accursed lake stumbling over boulders of basanite and ledges that were sharp with verdigris-covered metals; floundering in pits of salt, on terraces wrought by the receding tide in ancient æons, I fled as a man flies from dream to baleful dream of some cacodemoniacal night. At whiles there was a cold whisper in my ear, which did not come from the wind of my flight; and looking back as I reached one of the upper terraces, I perceived a singular shadow that ran pace by pace with my own. This shadow was not the shadow of man nor ape nor any known beast; the head was too grotesquely elongated, the squat body too gibbous; and I was unable to determine whether the shadow possessed five legs, or whether what appeared to be the fifth was merely a tail.

Terror lent me new strength, and I had reached the hilltop when I dared to look back again. But still the fantastic shadow kept pace by pace with mine; and now I caught a curious and utterly sickening odour, foul as the odour of bats who have hung in a charnel-house amid the mould of corruption. I ran for leagues, while the red sun slanted above the asteroidal mountains to the west; and the weird shadow lengthened with mine but kept always at the same distance behind me.

An hour before sunset I came to a circle of small pillars that rose miraculously unbroken amid ruins that were like a vast pile of potsherds. As I passed among these pillars I heard a whimper, like the whimper of some fierce animal, between rage and fear, and saw that the shadow had not followed me within the circle. I stopped and waited, conjecturing at once that I had found a sanctuary my unwelcome familiar would not dare to enter; and in this the action of the shadow confirmed me, for the Thing hesitated, then ran about the circle of columns, pausing often between them; and, whimpering all the while, at last went away and disappeared in the desert toward the setting sun.

For a full half hour I did not dare to move; then, the imminence of night, with all its probabilities of fresh terror, urged me to push on as far as I could to the north. For I was now in the very heart of Yondo where demons or phantoms might dwell who would not respect the sanctuary of the unbroken columns.

Now, as I toiled on, the sunlight altered strangely; for the red orb, nearing the mounded horizon, sank and smouldered in a belt of miasmal haze, where floating dust from all the shattered fanes and necropoli of Yondo was mixed with evil vapors coiling skyward from black enormous gulfs lying beyond the utmost rim of the world. In that light, the entire waste, the rounded mountains, the serpentine hills, the lost cities, were drenched with phantasmal and darkening scarlet.

Then, out of the north, where shadows mustered, there came a curious figure — a tall man fully caparisoned in chain-mail — or, rather, what I assumed to be a man. As the figure approached me, clanking dismally at each step on the sharded ground, I saw that its armour was of brass mottled with verdigris; and a casque of the same metal furnished with coiling horns and a serrate comb, rose high above its head. I say its head, for the sunset was darkening, and I could not see clearly at any distance; but when the apparition came abreast, I perceived that there was no face beneath the brows of the bizarre helmet whose empty edges were outlined for a moment against the smouldering light. Then the figure passed on, still clanking dismally, and vanished.

But on its heels, ere the sunset faded, there came a second apparition, striding with incredible strides and halting when it loomed almost upon me in the red twilight — the monstrous mummy of some ancient king, still crowned with untarnished gold, but turning to my gaze a visage that more than time or the worm had wasted. Broken swathings flapped about the skeleton legs, and above the crown that was set with sapphires and orange rubies, a black Something swayed and nodded horribly; but, for an instant, I did not dream what it was. Then, in its middle, two oblique and scarlet eyes opened and glowed like hellish coals, and two ophidian fangs glittered in an apelike mouth. A squat, furless, shapeless head on a neck of disproportionate extent leaned unspeakably down and whispered in the mummy's ear. Then, with one stride, the titanic lich took half the distance between us, and from out the folds of the tattered sere-cloth a gaunt arm arose, and fleshless, taloned fingers laden with glowering gems, reached out and fumbled for my throat . . .

Back, back through æons of madness and dread, in a prone, precipitate flight, I ran from those fumbling fingers that hung always on the dusk behind me, back, back forever, unthinking, unhesitating, to all the abominations I had left; back in the thickening twilight toward the nameless and sharded ruins, the haunted lake, the forest of evil cacti, and the cruel and cynical inquisitors of Ong who waited my return.

The Testament of Athammaus

It has become needful for me, who am no wielder of the stylus of bronze or the pen of calamus, and whose only proper tool is the long, double-handed sword, to indite this account of the curious and lamentable happenings which foreran the universal desertion of Commoriom by its king and its people. This I am well-fitted to do, for I played a signal part in these happenings; and I left the city only when all the others had gone.

Now Commoriom, as everyone knows, was afore-time the resplendent, high-built capital, and the marble and granite crown of all Hyperborea. But, concerning the cause of its abandonment, there are now so many war-ring legends and so many tales of a false and fabulous character, that I, who am old in years and triply old in horrors, I, who have grown weary with no less than eleven lustrums of public service, am compelled to write this record of the truth ere it fade utterly from the tongues and memories of men. And this I do, though the telling thereof will include a confession of my one defeat, my one failure in the dutiful administration of a com-mitted task.

For those who will read the narrative in future years, and haply in future lands, I shall now introduce myself. I am Athammaus, the chief headsman of Uzuldaroum, who held formerly the same office in Commoriom. My father, Manghai Thal, was headsman before me; and the sires of my father, even to the mythic generations of the primal kings, have wielded the great copper sword of justice on the block of *eighon*-wood.

Forgive an aged man if he seem to dwell, as is the habit of the old, among the youthful recollections that

18

have gathered to themselves the kingly purple of removed horizons and the strange glory that illumines irre-
trievable things. Lo! I am made young again when I recall
Commoriom, when in this grey city of the sunken years I
behold in retrospect her walls that looked mountain-
ously down upon the jungle, and the alabastrine multitude of her heaven-fretting spires. Opulent among cities,
and superb and magisterial, and paramount over all was
Commoriom, to whom tribute was given from the shores
of the Atlantean sea to that sea in which is the immense
continent of Mu; to whom the traders came from utmost
Thulan that is walled on the north with unknown ice, and
from the southern realm of Tscho Vulpanomi which ends
in a lake of boiling asphaltum. Ah! proud and lordly was
Commoriom, and her humblest dwellings were more
than the palaces of other cities. And it was not, as men
fable nowadays, because of that maundering prophecy
once uttered by the White Sybil from the isle of snow
which is named Polarion, that her splendor and spaciousness was delivered over to the spotted vines of the
jungle and the spotted snakes. Nay, it was because of a
direr thing than this, and a tangible horror against which
the law of kings, the wisdom of hierophants and the
sharpness of swords were alike impotent. Ah! not lightly
was she overcome, not easily were her defenders driven
forth. And though others forget, or haply deem her no
more than a vain and dubitable tale, I shall never cease to
lament Commoriom.

My sinews have dwindled grievously now; and
Time has drunken stealthily from my veins; and has
touched my hair with the ashes of suns extinct. But in the
days whereof I tell, there was no braver and more stal-
wart headsman than I in the whole of Hyperborea; and
my name was a red menace, a loudly spoken warning to
the evil-doers of the forest and the town, and the savage

robbers of uncouth outland tribes. Wearing the blood-bright purple of my office, I stood each morning in the public square where all might attend and behold, and performed for the edification of all men my allotted task. And each day the tough, golden-ruddy copper of the huge crescent blade was darkened not once but many times with a rich and winelike sanguine. And because of my never-faltering arm, my infallible eye, and the clean blow which there was never any necessity to repeat, I was much honored by the King Loquamethros and by the populace of Commoriom.

I remember well, on account of their more than unique atrocity, the earliest rumors that came to me in my active life regarding the outlaw Knygathin Zhaum. This person belonged to an obscure and highly unpleasant people called the Voormis, who dwelt in the black Eiglophian Mountains at a full day's journey from Commoriom, and inhabited according to their tribal custom the caves of ferine animals less savage than themselves, which they had slain or otherwise dispossessed. They were generally looked upon as more beastlike than human, because of their excessive hairiness and the vile, ungodly rites and usages to which they were addicted. It was mainly from among these beings that the notorious Knygathin Zhaum had recruited his formidable band, who were terrorizing the hills subjacent to the Eiglophian Mountains with daily deeds of the most infamous and iniquitous rapine. Wholesale robbery was the least of their crimes; and mere anthropophagism was far from being the worst.

It will readily be seen, from this, that the Voormis were a somewhat aboriginal race, with an ethnic heritage of the darkest and most revolting type. And it was commonly said that Knygathin Zhaum himself possessed an even murkier strain of ancestry than the others, being related on the maternal side to that queer, non-anthropomorphic god, Tsathoggua, who was worshipped so widely during the subhuman cycles. And there were those who whispered of even stranger blood (if one could properly call it blood) and a monstrous linkage with the swart Protean spawn that had come down with Tsathoggua from elder worlds and exterior dimensions where physiology and geometry had both assumed an altogether inverse trend of development. And, because of this mingling of ultra-cosmic strains, it was said that the body of Knygathin Zhaum, unlike his shaggy, umber-colored fellow tribesmen, was hairless from crown to heel and was pied with great spots of black and yellow; and moreover he himself was reputed to exceed all others in his cruelty and cunning.

For a long time this execrable outlaw was no more to me than an horrific name; but inevitably I thought of him with a certain professional interest. There were many who believed him invulnerable by any weapon, and who told of his having escaped in a manner which none could elucidate from more than one dungeon whose walls were not to be scaled or pierced by mortal beings. But of course I discounted all such tales, for my official experience had never yet included anyone with properties or abilities of a like sort. And I knew well the superstitiousness of the vulgar multitude.

From day to day new reports reached me amid the preoccupations of never-slighted duty. This noxious marauder was not content with the seemingly ample sphere of operations afforded by his native mountains and the outlying hill-regions with their fertile valleys and well-peopled towns. His forays became bolder and more extensive; till one night he descended on a village so near to Commoriom that it was usually classed as a suburb. Here he and his feculent crew committed numerous deeds of an unspecifiable enormity; and bearing with them many of the villagers for purposes even less designable, they retired to their caves in the glassy-walled Eiglophian peaks ere the ministers of justice could overtake them.

It was this audaciously offensive act which prompted the law to exert its full power and vigilance against Knygathin Zhaum. Before that, he and his men had been left to the local officers of the countryside; but now his misdeeds were such as to demand the rigorous attention of the constabulary of Commoriom. Henceforth all his movements were followed as closely as possible; the towns where he might descend were strictly guarded; and traps were set everywhere.

Even thus, Knygathin Zhaum contrived to evade capture for month after month; and all the while he repeated his far-flung raids with an embarrassing frequency. It was almost by chance, or through his own foolhardiness, that he was eventually taken in broad daylight on the highway near the city's outskirts. Contrary to all expectation, in view of his renowned ferocity, he made no resistance whatever; but finding himself surrounded by mailed archers and billbearers, he yielded to them at once with an oblique, enigmatic smile—a smile that troubled for many nights thereafter the dreams of all who were present.

For reasons which were never explained, he was altogether alone when taken; and none of his fellows were captured either coincidentally or subsequently. Nevertheless, there was much excitement and jubilation in Commoriom, and everyone was curious to behold the dreaded outlaw. More even than others, perhaps, I felt the stirrings of interest; for upon me, in due course, the proper decapitation of Knygathin Zhaum would devolve.

From hearing the hideous rumors and legends whose nature I have already outlined, I was prepared for something out of the ordinary in the way of criminal personality. But even at first sight, when I watched him as he was borne to prison through a moiling crowd, Knygathin Zhaum surpassed the most sinister and disagreeable anticipations. He was naked to the waist, and wore the fulvous hide of some long-haired animal which hung in filthy tatters to his knees. Such details, however, contributed little to those elements in his appearance which revolted and even shocked me. His limbs, his body, his lineaments were outwardly formed like those of aboriginal man; and one might even have allowed for his utter hairlessness, in which there was a remote and blasphemously caricatural suggestion of the shaven priest; and even the broad, formless mottling of his skin, like that of a huge boa, might somehow have been glossed over as a rather extravagant peculiarity of pigmentation. It was something else, it was the unctuous, verminous ease, the undulant litheness and fluidity of his every movement, seeming to hint at an inner structure and vertebration that were less than human—or, one might almost have said, a sub-ophidian lack of all bony framework—which made me view the captive, and also my incumbent task, with an unparallelable distaste. He seemed to slither rather than walk; and the very fashion of his jointure, the placing of knees, hips, elbows and shoulders, appeared arbitrary and factitious. One felt that the outward semblance of humanity was a mere concession to anatomical convention; and that his corporeal formation might easily have assumed— and might still assume at any instant—the unheard-of outlines and concept-defying dimensions that prevail in trans-galactic worlds. Indeed, I could now believe the outrageous tales concerning his ancestry. And with equal horror and curiosity I wondered what the stroke of justice would reveal, and what noisome, mephitic ichor would befoul the impartial sword in lieu of honest blood.

It is needless to record in circumstantial detail the process by which Knygathin Zhaum was tried and condemned for his manifold enormities. The workings of the law were implacably swift and sure, and their equity permitted of no quibbling or delay. The captive was confined in an oubliette below the main dungeons—a cell hewn in the basic, Archean gneiss at a profound depth, with no entrance other than a hole through which he was lowered and drawn up by means of a long rope and windlass. This hole was lidded with a huge block and was guarded day and night by a dozen men-at-arms. However, there was no attempt at escape on the part of Knygathin Zhaum: indeed, he seemed unnaturally resigned to his prospective doom.

To me, who have always been possessed of a strain of prophetic intuition, there was something overtly ominous in this unlooked-for resignation. Also, I did not like the demeanor of the prisoner during his trial. The silence which he had preserved at all times following his capture and incarceration was still maintained before his judges. Though interpreters who knew the harsh, sibilant Eiglophian dialect were provided, he would make no answer to questions; and he offered no defense. Least of all did I like the unabashed and unblinking manner in which he received the final pronouncement of death which was uttered in the high court of Commoriom by eight judges in turn and solemnly reaffirmed at the end by King Loquamethros. After that, I looked well to the sharpening of my sword, and promised myself that I would concentrate all the resources of a brawny arm and a flawless manual artistry upon the forthcoming execution.

My task was not long deferred, for the usual interval

of a fortnight between condemnation and decapitation had been shortened to three days in view of the suspicious peculiarities of Knygathin Zhaum and the heinous magnitude of his proven crimes.

On the morning appointed, after a night that had been rendered dismal by a long-drawn succession of the most abominable dreams, I went with my unfailing punctuality to the block of *eighon*-wood, which was situated with geometrical exactness in the center of the main square. Here a huge crowd had already gathered; and the clear amber sun blazed royally down on the silver and nacarat of court dignitaries, the hodden of merchants and artisans, and the rough pelts that were worn by outland people.

With a like punctuality, Knygathin Zhaum soon appeared amid his entourage of guards, who surrounded him with a bristling hedge of bill-hooks and lances and tridents. At the same time, all the outer avenues of the city, as well as the entrances to the square, were guarded by massed soldiery, for it was feared that the uncaught members of the desperate outlaw band might make an effort to rescue their infamous chief at the last moment.

Amid the unremitting vigilance of his warders, Knygathin Zhaum came forward, fixing upon me the intent but inexpressive gaze of his lidless, ochre-yellow eyes, in which a face-to-face scrutiny could discern no pupils. He knelt down beside the block, presenting his mottled nape without a tremor. As I looked upon him with a calculating eye, and made ready for the lethal stroke, I was impressed more powerfully and more disagreeably than ever by the feeling of a loathsome, underlying plasticity, an invertebrate structure, nauseous and non-terrestrial, beneath his impious mockery of human form. And I could not help perceiving also the air of abnormal coolness, of abstract, impenetrable cynicism, that was maintained by all his parts and members. He was like a torpid snake, or some huge liana of the jungle, that is wholly unconscious of the shearing axe.

I was well aware that I might be dealing with things which were beyond the ordinary province of a public headsman; but nathless I lifted the great sword in a clean, symmetrically flashing arc, and brought it down on the piebald nape with all of my customary force and address.

Necks differ in the sensations which they afford to one's hand beneath the penetrating blade. In this case, I can only say that the sensation was not such as I have grown to associate with the cleaving of any known animal substance. But I saw with relief that the blow had been successful: the head of Knygathin Zhaum lay cleanly severed on the porous block, and his body sprawled on the pavement without even a single quiver of departing animation. As I had expected, there was no blood—only a black, tarry, fetid exudation, far from copious, which ceased in a few minutes and vanished utterly from my sword and from the *eighon*-wood. Also, the inner anatomy which the blade had revealed was devoid of all legitimate vertebration. But to all appearance Knygathin Zhaum had yielded up his obscene life; and the sentence of King Loquamethros and the eight judges of Commoriom had been fulfilled with a legal precision.

Proudly but modestly I received the applause of the waiting multitudes, who bore willing witness to the consummation of my official task and were loudly jubilant over the dead scourge. After seeing that the remains of Knygathin Zhaum were given into the hands of the public grave-diggers, who always disposed of such offal, I left the square and returned to my home, since no other decapitations had been set for that day. My conscience was serene, and I felt that I had acquitted myself worthily in the performance of a far from pleasant duty.

Knygathin Zhaum, as was the custom in dealing with the bodies of the most nefarious criminals, was interred with contumelious haste in a barren field outside the city where people cast their orts and rubbish. He was left in an unmarked and unmounded grave between two middens. The power of the law had now been amply vindicated; and everyone was satisfied, from Loquamethros himself to the villagers that had suffered from the depredations of the deceased outlaw.

I retired that night, after a bounteous meal of *suvana*-fruit and *djongua*-beans, well-irrigated with *foum*-wine. From a moral standpoint, I had every reason to sleep the sleep of the virtuous; but, even as on the preceding night, I was made the victim of one cacodemoniacal dream after another. Of these dreams, I recall only their pervading, unifying consciousness of insufferable suspense, of monotonously cumulative horror without shape or name; and the ever-torturing sentiment of vain repetition and dark, hopeless toil and frustration. Also, there is a half-memory, which refuses to assume any approach to visual form, of things that were never intended for human perception or human cogitation; and the aforesaid sentiment, and all the horror, were dimly but indissolubly bound up with these.

Awaking unrefreshed and weary from what seemed an æon of thankless endeavor, of treadmill bafflement, I could only impute my nocturnal sufferings to the *djongua*-beans; and decided that I must have eaten all too liberally of these nutritious viands. Mercifully, I did not suspect in my dreams the dark, portentous symbolism that was soon to declare itself.

Now must I write the things that are formidable unto Earth and the dwellers of Earth; the things that exceed all human or terrene regimen; that subvert reason; that mock the dimensions and defy biology. Dire is the tale; and, after seven lustrums, the tremor of an olden fear still agitates my hand as I write.

But of such things I was still oblivious when I sallied forth that morning to the place of execution, where three criminals of a quite average sort, whose very cephalic contours I have forgotten along with their offenses, were to meet their well-deserved doom beneath my capable arm. Howbeit, I had not gone far when I heard an unconscionable uproar that was spreading swiftly from street to street, from alley to alley throughout Commoriom. I distinguished a myriad cries of rage, horror, fear and lamentation that were seemingly caught up and repeated by everyone who chanced to be abroad at that hour. Meeting some of the citizenry, who were plainly in a state of the most excessive agitation and were still continuing their outcries, I inquired the reason of all this clamor. And thereupon I learned from them that Knygathin Zhaum, whose illicit career was presumably at an end, had now reappeared and had signalized the unholy miracle of his return by the commission of a most appalling act on the main avenue before the very eyes of early passers! He had seized a respectable seller of *djongua*-beans, and had proceeded instantly to devour his victim *alive*, without heeding the blows, bricks, arrows, javelins, cobblestones and curses that were rained upon him by the gathering throng and by the police. It was only when he had satisfied his atrocious appetite, that he suffered the police to lead him away, leaving little more than the bones and raiment of the *djongua*-seller to mark the spot of this outrageous happening. Since the case was without legal parallel, Knygathin Zhaum had been thrown once more into the oubliette below the city dungeons, to await the will of Loquamethros and the eight judges.

The exceeding discomfiture, the profound embarrassment felt by myself, as well as by the people and the magistracy of Commoriom, can well be imagined. As everyone bore witness, Knygathin Zhaum had been efficiently beheaded and buried according to the customary ritual; and his resurrection was not only against nature but involved a most contumelious and highly mystifying breach of the law. In fact, the legal aspects of the case were such as to render necessary the immediate passing of a special statute, calling for rejudgment, and allowing re-execution, of such malefactors as might thus-wise return from their lawful graves. Apart from all this, there was general consternation; and even at that early date, the more ignorant and more religious among the towns-folk were prone to regard the matter as an omen of some impending civic calamity.

As for me, my scientific turn of mind, which repudiated the supernatural, led me to seek an explanation of the problem in the non-terrestrial side of Knygathin Zhaum's ancestry. I felt sure that the forces of an alien biology, the properties of a trans-stellar life-substance, were somehow involved.

With the spirit of the true investigator, I summoned the grave-diggers who had interred Knygathin Zhaum and bade them lead me to his place of sepulture in the refuse-grounds. Here a most singular condition disclosed itself. The earth had not been disturbed, apart from a deep hole at one end of the grave, such as might have been made by a large rodent. No body of human size, or, at least, of human form, could possibly have emerged from this hole. At my command, the diggers removed all the loose soil, mingled with potsherds and other rubbish, which they had heaped upon the beheaded outlaw. When they reached the bottom, nothing was found but a slight stickiness where the corpse had lain; and this, along with an odour of ineffable foulness which was its concomitant, soon dissipated itself in the open air.

Baffled, and more mystified than ever, but still sure that the enigma would permit of some natural solution, I awaited the new trial. This time, the course of justice was even quicker and less given to quibbling than before. The prisoner was again condemned, and the time of decapitation was delayed only till the following morn. A proviso concerning burial was added to the sentence: the remains were to be sealed in a strong wooden sarcophagus, the sarcophagus was to be inhumed in a deep pit in the solid stone, and the pit filled with massy boulders. These measures, it was felt, should serve amply to restrain the unwholesome and irregular inclinations of this obnoxious miscreant.

When Knygathin Zhaum was again brought before me, amid a redoubled guard and a throng that overflowed the square and all of the outlying avenues, I viewed him with profound concern and with more than my former repulsion. Having a good memory for anatomic details, I noticed some odd changes in his physique. The huge splotches of dull black and sickly yellow that had covered him from head to heel were now somewhat differently distributed. The shifting of the facial blotches, around the eyes and mouth, had given him an expression that was both grim and sardonic to an unbearable degree. Also, there was a perceptible *shortening* of his neck, though the place of cleavage and reunion, midway between head and shoulders, had left no mark whatever. And looking at his limbs, I discerned other and more subtle changes. Despite my acumen in physical matters, I found myself unwilling to speculate regarding the processes that might underlie these alterations; and still less did I wish to surmise the problematic results of their continuation, if such should ensue. Hoping fervently that Knygathin Zhaum and the vile, flagitious properties of his unhallowed carcass would now be brought to a permanent end, I raised the sword of justice high in air and smote with heroic might.

Once again, as far as mortal eye was able to determine, the effects of the shearing blow were all that could be desired. The head rolled forward on the *eighon*-wood, and the torso and its members fell and lay supinely on the maculated flags. From a legal viewpoint, this doubly nefarious malefactor was now twice-dead.

Howbeit, this time I superintended in person the disposal of the remains, and saw to the bolting of the fine sarcophagus of *apha*-wood in which they were laid, and the filling with chosen boulders of the ten-foot pit into which the sarcophagus was lowered. It required three men to lift even the least of these boulders. We all felt that the irrepressible Knygathin Zhaum was due for a quietus.

Alas for the vanity of earthly hopes and labors! The morrow came with its unspeakable, incredible tale of renewed outrage: once more the weird, semi-human offender was abroad, once more his anthropophagic lust had taken toll from among the honorable denizens of Commoriom. He had eaten no less a personage than one of the eight judges; and, not satisfied with picking the bones of this rather obese individual, had devoured by way of dessert the more outstanding facial features of one of the police who had tried to deter him from finishing his main course. All this, as before, was done amid the frantic protests of a great throng. After a final nibbling at the scant vestiges of the unfortunate constable's left ear, Knygathin Zhaum had seemed to experience a feeling of repletion and had suffered himself to be led docilely away once more by the jailers.

I, and the others who had helped me in the arduous toils of entombment, were more than astounded when we heard the news. And the effect on the general public was indeed deplorable. The more superstitious and timid began leaving the city forthwith; and there was much revival of forgotten prophecies; and much talk among the various priesthoods anent the necessity of placating with liberal sacrifice their mystically angered gods and eidolons. Such nonsense I was wholly able to disregard; but, under the circumstances, the persistent return of Knygathin Zhaum was no less alarming to science than to religion.

We examined the tomb, if only as a matter of form; and found that certain of the superincumbent boulders had been displaced in such a manner as to admit the outward passage of a body with the lateral dimensions of some large snake or muskrat. The sarcophagus, with its metal bolts, was bursten at one end; and we shuddered to think of the immeasurable force that must have been employed in its disruption.

Because of the way in which the case overpassed all known biologic laws, the formalities of civil law were now waived; and I, Athammaus, was called upon that same day before the sun had reached its meridian, and was solemnly charged with the office of re-beheading Knygathin Zhaum at once. The interment or other disposal of the remains was left to my discretion; and the local soldiery and constabulary were all placed at my command, if I should require them.

Deeply conscious of the honor thus implied, and sorely perplexed but undaunted, I went forth to the scene of my labors. When the criminal reappeared, it was obvious not only to me but to everyone that his physical personality, in achieving this new recrudescence, had undergone a most salient change. His mottling had developed more than a suggestion of some startling and repulsive pattern; and his human characteristics had yielded to the inroads of an unearthly distortion. The head was joined to the shoulders almost without the intermediation of a neck; the eyes were set diagonally in a face with oblique bulgings and flattenings; the nose and mouth were showing a tendency to displace each other; and there were still further alterations which I shall not specify, since they involved an abhorrent degradation of man's noblest and most distinctive corporeal members. I shall, however, mention the strange, pendulous formations, like annulated dewlaps or wattles, into which his kneecaps had evolved. Nathless, it was Knygathin Zhaum himself who stood (if one could dignify the fashion of his carriage by that word) before the block of justice.

Because of the virtual non-existence of a nape, the third beheading called for a precision of eye and a nicety of hand which, in all likelihood, no other headsman than myself could have shown. I rejoice to say that my skill was adequate to the demand thus made upon it; and once again the culprit was shorn of his vile cephaloid appendage. But if the blade had gone even a little to either side, the dismemberment entailed would have been technically of another sort than decapitation.

The laborious care with which I and my assistants conducted the third inhumation was indeed deserving of success. We laid the body in a strong sarcophagus of bronze, and the head in a second but smaller sarcophagus of the same material. The lids were then soldered down with molten metal; and after this the two sarcophagi were conveyed to opposite parts of Commoriom. The one containing the body was buried at a great depth beneath monumental masses of stone; but that which enclosed the head I left uninterred, proposing to watch over it all night in company with a guard of armed men. I also appointed a numerous guard to keep vigil above the burial-place of the body.

Night came; and with seven trusty trident-bearers I went forth to the place where we had left the smaller of the two sarcophagi. This was in the courtyard of a deserted mansion amid the suburbs, far from the haunts of the populace. For weapons, I myself wore a short falchion and carried a great bill. We took along a plentiful supply of torches, so that we might not lack for light in our gruesome vigil; and we lit several of them at once and stuck them in crevices between the flagstones of the court, in such wise that they formed a circle of lurid flames about the sarcophagus.

We had also brought with us an abundance of the crimson *foum*-wine in leathern bottles, and dice of mammoth-ivory with which to beguile the black nocturnal hours; and eyeing our charge with a casual but careful vigilance, we applied ourselves discreetly to the wine and began to play for small sums of no more than five *pazoors*, as is the wont of good gamblers till they have taken their opponents' measure.

The darkness deepened apace; and in the square of sapphire overhead, to which the illumination of our torches had given a jetty tinge, we saw Polaris and the red planets that looked down for the last time upon Commoriom in her glory. But we dreamed not of the nearness of disaster, but jested bravely and drank in ribald mockery to the monstrous head that was now so securely coffined and so remotely sundered from its odious body. And the wine passed and repassed among us; and its rosy spirit mounted in our brains; and we played for bolder stakes; and the game quickened to a goodly frenzy.

I know not how many stars had gone over us in the smoky heavens, nor how many times I had availed myself of the ever-circling bottles. But I remember well that I had won no less than ninety *pazoors* from the trident-bearers, who were all swearing lustily and loudly as they strove in vain to stem the tide of my victory. I, as well as the others, had wholly forgotten the object of our vigil.

The sarcophagus containing the head was one that had been primarily designed for the reception of a small child. Its present use, one might have argued, was a sinful and sacrilegious waste of fine bronze; but nothing else of proper size and adequate strength was available at the time. In the mounting fervor of the game, as I have hinted, we had all ceased to watch this receptacle; and I shudder to think how long there may have been something visibly or even audibly amiss before the unwonted and terrifying behavior of the sarcophagus was forced upon our attention. It was the sudden, loud, metallic clangor, like that of a smitten gong or shield, which made us realize that all things were not as they should have been; and turning unanimously in the direction of the sound, we saw that the sarcophaghus was heaving and pitching in a most unseemly fashion amid its ring of flaring torches. First on one end or corner, then on another, it danced and pirouetted, clanging resonantly all the while on the granite pavement.

The true horror of the situation had scarcely seeped into our brains, ere a new and even more ghastly development occurred. We saw that the casket was bulging ominously at top and sides and bottom, and was rapidly losing all similitude to its rightful form. Its rectangular outlines swelled and curved and were horribly erased as in the changes of a nightmare, till the thing became a slightly oblong sphere; and then, with a most appalling noise, it began to split at the welded edges of the lid, and burst violently asunder. Through the long, ragged rift there poured in hellish ebullition a dark, ever-swelling mass of incognizable matter, frothing as with the venomous foam of a million serpents, hissing as with the yeast of fermenting wine, and putting forth here and there great sooty-looking bubbles that were large as pig-bladders. Overturning several of the torches, it rolled in an inundating wave across the flag-stones and we all sprang back in the most abominable fright and stupefaction to avoid it.

Cowering against the rear wall of the courtyard, while the overthrown torches flickered wildly and smokily, we watched the remarkable actions of the mass, which had paused as if to collect itself, and was now sub-siding like a sort of infernal dough. It shrank, it fell in, till after awhile its dimensions began to reapproach those of the encoffined head, though they still lacked any true semblance of its shape. The thing became a round, black-ish ball, on whose palpitating surface the nascent out-lines of random features were limned with the flatness of a drawing. There was one lidless eye, tawny, pupilless and phosphoric, that stared upon us from the center of the ball while the thing appeared to be making up its mind. It lay still for more than a minute; then, with a cata-pulting bound, it sprang past us toward the open en-trance of the courtyard, and disappeared from our ken on the midnight streets.

Despite our amazement and disconcertion, we were able to note the general direction in which it had gone. This, to our further terror and confoundment, was toward the portion of Commoriom in which the body of Knygathin Zhaum had been intombed. We dared not conjecture the meaning of it all, and the prob-able outcome. But, though there were a million fears and apprehensions to deter us, we seized our weapons and followed on the path of that unholy head with all the immediacy and all the forthrightness of motion which a goodly cargo of *foum*-wine would permit.

No one other than ourselves was abroad at an hour when even the most dissolute revellers had either gone home or had succumbed to their potations under tavern tables. The streets were dark, and were somehow drear and cheerless; and the stars above them were half stifled as by the invading mist of a pestilential miasma. We went on, following a main street, and the pavements echoed to our tread in the stillness with a hollow sound, as if the solid stone beneath them had been honeycombed with mausolean vaults in the interim of our weird vigil.

In all our wanderings, we found no sign of that supremely noxious and execrable thing which had issued from the riven sarcophagus. Nor, to our relief, and contrary to all our fears, did we encounter anything of an allied or analogous nature, such as might be abroad if our surmises were correct. But, near the central square of Commoriom, we met with a number of men, carrying bills and tridents and torches, who proved to be the guards I had posted that evening above the tomb of Knygathin Zhaum's body. These men were in a state of pitiable agitation; and they told us a fearsome tale, of how the deep-hewn tomb and the monumental blocks of stone that were piled within it had heaved as with the throes of earthquake; and of how a python-shapen mass of frothing and hissing matter had poured forth from amid the blocks and had vanished into the darkness toward Commoriom. In return, we told them of that which had happened during our vigil in the courtyard; and we all agreed that a great foulness, a thing more baneful than beast or serpent, was again loose and ravening in the night. And we spoke only in shocked whispers of what the morrow might declare.

Uniting our forces, we searched the city, combing cautiously its alleys and its thoroughfares and dreading with the dread of brave men the dark, iniquitous spawn on which the light of our torches might fall at any turn or in any nook or portal. But the search was vain; and the stars grew faint above us in a livid sky; and the dawn came in among the marble spires with a glimmering of ghostly silver; and a thin, phantasmal amber was sifted on walls and pavements.

Soon there were footsteps other than ours that echoed through the town; and one by one the familiar clangors and clamors of life awoke. Early passers appeared; and the sellers of fruits and milk and legumes came in from the countryside. But of that which we sought there was still no trace.

We went on, while the city continued to resume its matutinal activities around us. Then, abruptly, with no warning, and under circumstances that would have startled the most robust and affrayed the most valorous, we came upon our quarry. We were entering the square in which was the *eighon*-block whereon so many thousand miscreants had laid their piacular necks, when we heard an outcry of mortal dread and agony such as only one thing in the world could have occasioned. Hurrying on, we saw that two wayfarers, who had been crossing the square near the block of justice, were struggling and writhing in the clutch of an unequalled monster which both natural history and fable would have repudiated.

In spite of the baffling, ambiguous oddities which the thing displayed, we identified it as Knygathin Zhaum when we drew closer. The head, in its third reunion with that detestable torso, had attached itself in a semi-flattened manner to the region of the lower chest and diaphragm; and during the process of this novel coalescence, one eye had slipped away from all relation with its fellow or the head and was now occupying the navel, just below the embossment of the chin. Other and even more shocking alterations had occurred: the arms had lengthened into tentacles, with fingers that were like knots of writhing vipers; and where the head would normally have been, the shoulders had reared themselves to a cone-shaped eminence that ended in a cuplike mouth. Most fabulous and impossible of all, however, were the changes in the nether limbs: at each knee and hip, they had re-bifurcated into long, lithe proboscides that were lined with throated suckers. By making a combined use of its various mouths and members, the abnormality was devouring both of the hapless persons whom it had seized.

Drawn by the outcries, a crowd gathered behind us as we neared this atrocious tableau. The whole city seemed to fill with a well-nigh instantaneous clamor, an ever-swelling hubbub, in which the dominant note was one of supreme, all-devastating terror.

I shall not speak of our feelings as officers and men. It was plain to us that the ultra-mundane factors in Knygathin Zhaum's ancestry had asserted themselves with a hideously accelerative ratio, following his latest resurrection. But, maugre this, and the wholly stupendous enormity of the miscreation before us, we were still prepared to fulfill our duty and defend as best we could the helpless populace. I boast not of the heroism required: we were simple men, and should have done only that which we were visibly called upon to do.

We surrounded the monster, and would have assailed it immediately with our bills and tridents. But here an embarrassing difficulty disclosed itself: the creature before us had entwined itself so tortuously and inextricably with its prey, and the whole group was writhing and tossing so violently, that we could not use our weapons without grave danger of impaling or otherwise injuring our two fellow-citizens. At length, however, the strugglings and heavings grew less vehement, as the substance and life-blood of the men was consumed; and the loathsome mass of devourer and devoured became gradually quiescent.

Now, if ever, was our opportunity; and I am sure we should all have rallied to the attack, useless and vain as it would certainly have been. But plainly the monster had grown weary of all such trifling and would no longer submit himself to the petty annoyance of human molestation. As we raised our weapons and made ready to strike, the thing drew back, still carrying its vein-drawn, flaccid victims, and climbed upon the *eighon*-block. Here, before the eyes of all assembled, it began to swell in every part, in every member, as if it were inflating itself with a superhuman rancor and malignity. The rate at which the swelling progressed, and the proportions which the thing attained as it covered the block from sight and lapsed down on every side with undulating, inundating folds, would have been enough to daunt the heroes of remotest myth. The bloating of the main torso, I might add, was more lateral than vertical. When the abnormality began to present dimensions that were beyond those of any creature of this world, and to bulge aggressively toward us with a slow, interminable stretching of boalike arms, my valiant and redoubtable companions were scarcely to be censured for retreating. And even less can I blame the general population, who were now evacuating Commoriom in torrential multitudes, with shrill cries and wailings. Their flight was no doubt accelerated by the vocal sounds, which, for the first time during our observation, were being emitted by the monster. These sounds partook of the character of hissings more than anything else; but their volume was overpowering, their timbre was a torment and a nausea to the ear; and, worst of all, they were issuing not only from the diaphragmic mouth but from each of the various other oral openings or suckers which the horror had developed. Even I, Athammaus, drew back from those hissings and stood well beyond reach of the coiling serpentine fingers.

I am proud to say, however, that I lingered on the edge of the empty square for some time, with more than one backward and regretful glance. The thing that had been Knygathin Zhaum was seemingly content with its triumph; and it brooded supine and mountainous above the vanquished *eighon*-block. Its myriad hisses sank to a slow, minor sibilation such as might issue from a family of somnolent pythons; and it made no overt attempt to assail or even approach me. But seeing at last that the professional problem which it offered was quite insoluble; and divining moreover that Commoriom was by now entirely without a king, a judicial system, a constabulary or a people, I finally abandoned the doomed city and followed the others.

THE THIRD EPISODE
OF VATHEK

The Story of the Princess Zulkaïs and the Prince Kalilah

by William Beckford and Clark Ashton Smith

My Father, lord, can scarcely be unknown to you, inasmuch as the Caliph Motassem had entrusted to his care the fertile province of Masre. Nor would he have been unworthy of his exalted position if, in view of man's ignorance and weakness, an inordinate desire to control the future were not to be accounted an unpardonable error.

The Émir Abou Taher Achmed, however—for such was my father's name—was very far from recognizing this truth. Only too often did he seek to forestall Providence, and to direct the course of events in spite of the decrees of Heaven. Ah! terrible indeed are those decrees! Sooner or later their accomplishment is sure! Vainly do we seek to oppose them!

During a long course of years, everything flourished under my father's rule, and among the Émirs who have successfully administered that beautiful province, Abou Taher Achmed will not be forgotten. Following his speculative bent, he enlisted the services of certain experienced Nubians, born near the sources of the Nile, who had studied the stream throughout its course, and knew all its characteristics, and the properties of its waters; and, with their aid, he carried out his impious design of regulating the overflow of the river. Thus he covered the country with a too luxuriant vegetation, which left it afterwards exhausted. The people, always slaves to outward appearances, applauded his enterprises, worked indefatigably at the unnumbered canals with which he intersected the land, and, blinded by his successes, passed lightly over any unfortunate circumstances accompanying them. If, out of every ten ships that he sent forth to traffic, according to his fancy, a single ship came back richly freighted after a successful voyage, the wreck of the other nine was counted for nothing. Moreover, as, owing to his care and vigilance, commerce prospered under his rule, he was himself deceived as to his losses, and took to himself all the glory of his gains.

Soon Abou Taher Achmed came to be convinced that if he could recover the arts and sciences of the ancient Egyptians, his power would be unbounded. He believed that, in the remote ages of antiquity, men had appropriated to their own use some rays of the divine wisdom, and thus been enabled to work marvels, and he did not despair of bringing back once again that glorious time. For this purpose he caused search to be made, among the ruins abounding in the country, for the mysterious tablets which, according to the report of the Sages who swarmed in his court, would show how the arts and sciences in question were to be acquired, and also indicate the means of discovering hidden treasures, and subduing the Intelligences by which those treasures were guarded. Never before his time had any Mussulman puzzled his brains over hieroglyphics. Now, however, search was made, on his behalf, for hieroglyphics of every kind, in all quarters, in the remotest provinces, the strange symbols being faithfully copied on linen cloths. I have seen these cloths a thousand times, stretched out on the roofs of our palace. Nor could bees be more busy and assiduous about a bed of flowers than were the Sages about these painted sheets. But, as each Sage entertained a different opinion as to the meaning of what was there depicted, arguments were frequent, and quarrels ensued. Not only did the Sages spend the hours of daylight in prosecuting their researches, but the moon often shed its beams upon them while so occupied. They did not dare to light torches upon the terraced roofs, for fear of alarming the faithful Mussulmans, who were beginning to blame my father's veneration for an idolatrous antiquity, and regarded all these painted symbols, these figures, with a pious horror.

Meanwhile, the Émir, who would never have thought of neglecting any real matter of business however unimportant, for the pursuit of his strange studies, was by no means so particular with regard to his religious observances, and often forgot to perform the ablutions ordained by the law. The women of his harem did not fail to perceive this, but were afraid to speak, as, for one reason and another, their influence had considerably waned. But, on a certain day, Shaban, the chief of the eunuchs, who was very old and very pious, presented himself before his master, holding a ewer and golden basin, and said: "The waters of the Nile have been given for the cleansing of all our impurities; their source is in the clouds of heaven, not in the temples of idols; take and use those waters, for you stand in need of them."

The Émir, duly impressed by the action and speech of Shaban, yielded to his just remonstrances, and, instead of unpacking a large bale of painted cloths, which had just arrived from a far distance, ordered the eunuch to serve the day's collation in the Hall of the Golden Trellises, and to assemble there all his slaves, and all his birds—of which he kept a large number in aviaries of sandalwood.

Immediately the palace rang to the sound of instruments of music, and groups of slaves appeared, all dressed in their most attractive garments, and each leading in leash a peacock whiter than snow. One only of these slaves—whose slender and graceful form was a delight to the eye—had no bird in leash, and kept her veil down.

"Why this eclipse?" said the Émir to Shaban.

"Lord," answered he with joyful mien, "I am better than all your astrologers, for it is I who have discovered this lovely star. But do not imagine that she is yet within your reach; her father, the holy and venerable Iman Abzenderoud, will never consent to make you happy in the possession of her charms unless you perform your ablutions with greater regularity, and give the go-by to the Sages and their hieroglyphics."

My father, without replying to Shaban, ran to snatch away the veil that hid the countenance of Ghulendi Begum—for such was the name of Abzenderoud's daughter—and he did so with such violence that he nearly crushed two peacocks, and overturned several baskets of flowers. To this sudden heat succeeded a kind of ecstatic stupor. At last he cried: "How beautiful she is, how divine! Go, fetch at once the Iman of Soussouf—let the nuptial chamber be got ready, and all necessary preparations for our marriage be complete within one hour!"

"But, Lord," said Shaban, in consternation, "you forget that Ghulendi Begum cannot marry you without the consent of her father, who makes it a condition that you should abandon. . . ."

"What nonsense are you talking?" interrupted the Émir. "Do you think I am fool enough not to prefer this young virgin, fresh as the dew of the morning, to cartloads of hieroglyphics, mouldy and of the color of dead ashes? As to Abzenderoud, go and fetch him if you like—but quickly, for I shall certainly not wait a moment longer than I please."

"Hasten, Shaban," said Ghulendi Begum modestly, "hasten; you see that I am not here in case to make any very effectual resistance."

"It's my fault," mumbled the eunuch as he departed, "but I shall do what I can to rectify my error."

Accordingly he flew to find Abzenderoud. But that faithful servant of Allah had gone from home very early in the morning, and sought the open fields in order to pursue his pious investigations into the growth of plants and the life of insects. A deathlike pallor overspread his countenance when he saw Shaban swooping down upon him like a raven of ill omen, and heard him tell, in broken accents, how the Émir had promised nothing, and how he himself might well arrive too late to exact the pious conditions he had so deeply pondered. Nevertheless, the Iman did not lose courage, and reached my father's palace in a very few moments; but unfortunately he was by this time so out of breath that he sank down on a sofa, and remained for over an hour panting and breathless.

While all the eunuchs were doing their best to revive the holy man, Shaban had quickly gone up to the apartment assigned to Abou Taher Achmed's pleasures; but his zeal suffered some diminution when he saw the door guarded by two black eunuchs, who, brandishing their sabres, informed him that if he ventured to take one more step forward, his head would roll at his own feet. Therefore he had nothing better to do than to return to Abzenderoud, whose gaspings he regarded with wild and troubled eyes, lamenting the while over his own imprudence in bringing Ghulendi Begum within the Émir's power.

Notwithstanding the care my father was taking for the entertainment of the new sultana, he had heard something of the dispute between the black eunuchs and

Shaban, and had a fair notion of what was going on. As soon, therefore, as he judged it convenient, he came to find Abzenderoud in the Hall of the Golden Trellises, and presenting Ghulendi Begum to the holy man assured him that, while awaiting his arrival, he, the Émir, had made her his wife.

At these words, the Iman uttered a lamentable and piercing cry, which relieved the pressure on his chest; and, rolling his eyes in a fearful manner, he said to the new sultana: "Wretched woman, dost thou not know that rash and ill-considered acts lead ever to a miserable end? Thy father would have made thy lot secure; but thou hast not awaited the result of his efforts, or rather it is Heaven itself that mocks all human previsions. I ask nothing more of the Émir; let him deal with thee, and with his hieroglyphics, as he deems best! I foresee untold evils in the future; but I shall not be there to witness them. Rejoice for a while, intoxicated with thy pleasures. As for me, I call to my aid the Angel of Death, and hope, within three days, to rest in peace in the bosom of our great Prophet!"

After saying these words, he rose to his feet, tottering. His daughter strove in vain to hold him back. He tore his robe from her trembling hands. She fell fainting to the ground, and while the distracted Émir was striving to bring her back again to her senses, the obstinate Abzenderoud went muttering from the room.

At first it was thought that the holy man would not keep his vow quite literally, and would suffer himself to be comforted; but such was not the case. On reaching his own house, he began by stopping his ears with cotton wool, so as not to hear the clamor and adjuration of his friends; and then, having seated himself on the mats in his cell, with his legs crossed, and his head in his hands, he remained in that posture speechless, and taking no food; and finally, at the end of three days, expired according to his prayer. He was buried magnificently, and during the obsequies Shaban did not fail to manifest his grief by slashing his flesh without mercy, and soaking the earth with little rivulets of his blood; after which, having caused balm to be applied to his wounds, he returned to the duties of his office.

Meanwhile, the Émir had no small difficulty in assuaging the despair of Ghulendi Begum, and often cursed the hieroglyphics which had been its first efficient cause. At last his attentions touched the heart of the sultana. She regained her ordinary equability of spirits, and became pregnant; and everything returned to its accustomed order.

The Émir, his mind always dwelling on the magnificence of the ancient Pharaohs, built, after their manner, a palace with twelve pavilions—proposing, at an early date, to install in each pavilion a son. Unfortunately, his wives brought forth nothing but daughters. At each new birth he grumbled, gnashed his teeth, accused Mahomet of being the cause of his mishaps, and would have been altogether unbearable, if Ghulendi Begum had not found means to moderate his evil temper. She induced him to come every night into her apartment, where, by a thousand ingenious devices, she succeeded in introducing fresh air, while, in other parts of the palace, the atmosphere was stifling.

During her pregnancy my father never left the dais on which she reclined. This dais was set on a large and long gallery overlooking the Nile, and so disposed as to seem about on a level with the stream,—so close, too, that anyone reclining upon it could throw into the water the seeds of any pomegranate he might be eating. The best dancers, the most excellent magicians, were always about the palace. Every night pantomimes were performed to the light of a thousand golden lamps—lamps placed upon the floor so as to bring out the fineness and grace of the performers' feet. The dancers themselves cost my father immense sums in golden-fringed slippers and sandals a-glitter with jewelry; and, indeed, when they were all in motion together the effect was dazzling.

But notwithstanding this accumulation of splendors, the sultana passed very unhappy days on her dais. With the same indifference that a poor wretch tormented by sleeplessness watches the scintillations of the stars, so did she see pass before her eyes all this whirl of performers in their brilliancy and charm. Anon she would think of the wrath, that seemed almost prophetic, of her venerable father; anon she would deplore his strange and untimely end. A thousand times she would interrupt the choir of singers, crying: "Fate has decreed my ruin! Heaven will not vouchsafe me a son, and my husband will banish me from his sight!" The torment of her mind intensified the pain and discomfort attendant on her condition. My father, thereupon, was so greatly perturbed that, for the first time in his life, he made appeal to Heaven, and ordered prayers to be offered up in every mosque. Nor did he omit the giving of alms, for he caused it to be publicly announced that all beggars were to assemble in the largest court of the palace, and would there be served with rice, each according to his individual appetite. There followed such a crush every morning at the palace gates that the incomers were nearly suffocated. Mendicants swarmed in from all parts, by land, and by river. Whole villages would come down the stream on rafts. And the appetites of all were enormous; for the buildings which my father had erected, his costly pursuit of hieroglyphics, and his maintenance of the Sages, had caused some scarcity throughout the land.

Among those who came from a very far distance was

a man of an extreme age, and great singularity, by name Abou Gabdolle Guehaman, the hermit of the Great Sandy Desert. He was eight feet high, so ill-proportioned, and of a leanness so extreme, that he looked like a skeleton, and was hideous to behold. Nevertheless, this lugubrious and forbidden piece of human mechanism enshrined the most benevolent and religious spirit in the universe. With a voice of thunder he proclaimed the will of the Prophet, and said openly it was a pity that a prince who distributed rice to the poor, and in such great profusion, should be a lover of hieroglyphics. People crowded around him—the Imans, the Mullahs, the Muezins, did nothing but sing his praises. His feet, though ingrained with the sand of his native desert, were freely kissed. Nay, the very grains of the sand from his feet were gathered up, and treasured in caskets of amber.

One day he proclaimed the truth and the horror of the sciences of evil, in a voice so loud and resonant that the great standards set before the palace trembled. The terrible sound penetrated into the interior of the harem. The women and the eunuchs fainted away in the Hall of the Golden Trellises; the dancers stood with one foot arrested in the air; the mummers had not the courage to pursue their antics; the musicians suffered their instruments to fall to the ground; and Ghulendi Begum thought to die of fright as she lay on her dais.

Abou Taher Achmed stood astounded. His conscience smote him for his idolatrous proclivities, and during a few remorseful moments he thought that the Avenging Angel had come to turn him into stone—and not himself only but the people committed to his charge.

After standing for some time, upright, with arms uplifted, in the Gallery of the Daises, he called Shaban to him, and said: "The sun has not lost its brightness, the Nile flows peacefully in its bed, what means then this supernatural cry that has just resounded through my palace?"

"Lord," answered the pious eunuch, "this voice is the voice of Truth, and is spoken to you through the mouth of the venerable Abou Gabdolle Guehaman, the Hermit of the Sandy Desert, the most faithful, the most zealous, of the servants of the Prophet, who has, in nine days, journeyed three hundred leagues to make proof of your hospitality, and to impart to you the knowledge with which he is inspired. Do not neglect the teachings of a man who in wisdom, in piety, and in stature, surpasses the most enlightened, the most devout, and the most gigantic of the inhabitants of earth. All your people are in an ecstasy. Trade is at a standstill. The inhabitants of the city hasten to hear him, neglecting their wonted assemblies in the public gardens. The story-tellers are without hearers at the margins of the public fountains. Joussouf himself was not wiser than he, and had no greater knowledge of the future."

At these last words, the Émir was suddenly smitten with the desire of consulting Abou Gabdolle with regard to his family affairs, and particularly with regard to the great projects he entertained for the future advantage of his sons, who were not yet born. He deemed himself happy in being thus able to consult a living prophet; for, so far, it was only in the form of mummies that he had been brought into relation with these inspired personages. He resolved, therefore, to summon into his presence, nay, into his very harem, the extraordinary being now in question. Would not the Pharaohs have so dealt with the necromancers of their time, and was not he determined, in all circumstances, to follow the Pharaohs' example? He therefore graciously directed Shaban to go and fetch the holy man.

Shaban, transported with joy, hastened to communicate this invitation to the hermit, who, however, did not appear to be as much charmed by the summons as were the people at large. These latter filled the air with their acclamations, while Abou Gabdolle stood still, with his hands clasped, and his eyes uplifted to heaven, in a prophetic trance. From time to time he uttered the deepest sighs, and, after, remaining long rapt in holy contemplation, shouted out, in his voice of thunder: "Allah's will be done! I am but his creature. Eunuch, I am ready to follow thee. But let the doors of the palace be broken down. It is not meet for the servants of the Most High to bend their heads."

The people needed no second command. They all set hands to the work with a will, and in an instant the gateway, a piece of the most admirable workmanship, was utterly ruined.

At the sound of the breaking in of the doors, piercing cries arose within the harem. Abou Taher Achmed began to repent of his curiosity. Nevertheless, he ordered, though somewhat reluctantly, that the passages into the harem should be laid open to the holy giant, for he feared lest the enthusiastic adherents of the prophet should penetrate into the apartments occupied by the women, and containing the princely treasures. These fears were, however, vain, for the holy man had sent back his devout admirers. I have been assured that on their all kneeling to receive his blessing he said to them, in tones of the deepest solemnity: "Retire, remain peacefully in your dwellings, and be assured that, whatever happens, Abou Gabdolle Guehaman is prepared for every emergency." Then, turning towards the palace, he cried: "O domes of dazzling brilliancy, receive me, and may nothing ensue to tarnish your splendor."

Meanwhile, everything had been made ready within the harem. Screens had been duly ordered, the door-curtains had been drawn, and ample draperies hung before the daises in the long gallery that ran round the interior of the building—thus concealing from view the sultanas, and the princesses, their daughters.

Such elaborate preparations had caused a general ferment; and curiosity was at its height, when the hermit, trampling under foot the ruined fragments of the doorways, entered majestically into the Hall of the Golden Trellises. The magnificence of the palace did not even win from him a passing glance, his eyes remained fixed, mournfully, on the pavement at his feet. At last he penetrated into the great gallery of the women. These latter, who were not at all accustomed to the sight of creatures so lean, gaunt, and gigantic, uttered piercing cries, and loudly asked for essences and cordials to enable them to bear up against the apparition of such a phantasm.

The hermit paid not the smallest heed to the surrounding tumult. He was gravely pursuing his way, when the Émir came forward, and, taking him by the skirt of his garment, led him, with much ceremony, to the dais of the gallery which looked out upon the Nile. Basins of comfits and orthodox liquors were at once served; but though Abou Gabdolle Guehaman seemed to be dying of hunger, he refused to partake of these refreshments, saying that for ninety years he had drunk nothing but the dew of heaven, and eaten only the locusts of the desert. The Émir, who regarded this diet as conformable to what might properly be expected of a prophet, did not press him further, but at once entered into the question he had at heart, saying how much it grieved him to be without a male heir, notwithstanding all the prayers offered up to that effect, and the flattering hopes which the Imans had given him. "But now," he continued, "I am assured that this happiness will at last be mine. The Sages, the mediciners, predict it, and my own observations confirm their prognostications. It is not, therefore, with the purpose of consulting you with regard to the future that I have caused you to be summoned. It is for the purpose of obtaining your advice upon the education I should give to the son whose birth I am expecting or rather, to the two sons, for, without doubt, in recognition of my alms, Heaven will accord to the Sultana Ghulendi Begum a double measure of fertility, seeing that she is twice as large as women usually are on such occasions."

Without answering a word, the hermit mournfully shook his head three times.

My father, greatly astonished, asked if his anticipated good fortune was in any wise displeasing to the holy man.

"Ah! too blind prince," replied the hermit, uttering a cavernous sigh that seemed to issue from the grave itself, "why importune Heaven with rash prayers? Respect its decrees! It knows what is best for all men better than they do themselves. Woe be to you, and woe be to the son whom you will doubtless compel to follow in the perverse ways of your own beliefs, instead of submitting himself humbly to the guidance of Providence. If the great of this world could only foresee all the misfortunes they bring upon themselves, they would tremble in the midst of their splendor. Pharaoh recognized this truth, but too late. He pursued the children of Moussa despite the divine decrees, and died the death of the wicked. What can alms avail when the heart is in rebellion? Instead of asking the Prophet for an heir, to be led by you into the paths of destruction, those who have your welfare at heart should implore him to cause Ghulendi Begum to die—yes, to die before she brings into the world presumptuous creatures, whom your conduct will precipitate into the abyss! Once again I call upon you to

submit. If Allah's angel threatens to cut short the days of
the sultana, do not make appeal to your magicians to
ward off the fatal blow: let it fall, let her die! Tremble not
with wrath, Émir; harden not your heart! Once again call
to mind the fate of Pharaoh and the waters that swallowed him up!"

"Call them to mind yourself!" cried my father, foam-
ing with rage, and springing from the dais to run to the
aid of the sultana, who, having heard all, had fainted
away behind the curtains. "Remember that the Nile
flows beneath these windows, and that thou hast well
deserved that thy odious carcass should be hurled into its
waters!"

"I fear not," cried the gigantic hermit in turn; "the
prophet of Allah fears naught but himself," and he rose
on the tips of his toes and touched with his hands the
supports of the dome of the apartment.

"Ha! ha! thou fearest nothing," cried all the women
and eunuchs, issuing like tigers out of their den. "Accursed assassin, thou hast just brought our beloved mis-
tress to death's door, and yet fearest nothing! Go, and
become food for the monsters of the river!" Screaming
out these words, they threw themselves, all at once, on
Abou Gabdolle Guehaman, bore him down, strangled
him without pity, and cast his body through a dark grating into the Nile, which there lost itself obscurely among
the piers of iron.

The Émir, astonished by an act at once so sudden
and so atrocious, remained with his eyes fixed on the
waters; but the body did not again come to the surface;
and Shaban, who now appeared upon the scene, bewildered him with his cries. At last he turned to look upon
the perpetrators of the crime; but they had scattered in
every direction, and hidden behind the curtains of the
gallery, each avoiding the other, they were all over-

whelmed by the thought of what they had done.

Ghulendi, who had only come to herself in time to witness this scene of horror, was now in mortal anguish. Her convulsions, her agonizing cries, drew the Émir to her side. He bedewed her hand with tears. She opened her eyes wildly, and cried: "O Allah! Allah! put an end to a wretched creature who has already lived only too long, since she has been the cause of so terrible an outrage, and suffer not that she should bring into the world—"

"Stop, stop," interrupted the Émir, holding her hands which she was about to turn against herself, "thou shalt not die, and my children shall yet live to give the lie to that demented skeleton, worthy only of contempt. Let my Sages be summoned instantly. Let them use all their art to keep thy soul from flitting hence and to save from harm the fruit of thy body."

The Sages were convened accordingly. They demanded that one of the courts in the palace should be placed entirely at their disposal, and there began their operations, kindling a fire whose light penetrated into the gallery. The sultana rose from her couch, notwithstanding all the efforts made to restrain her, and ran to the balcony overlooking the Nile. The view from thence was lonely and drear. Not a single boat showed upon the surface of the stream. In the distance were discernible reaches of sand which the wind, from time to time, sent whirling into the air. The rays of the setting sun dyed the waters blood-red. Scarcely had the deepening twilight stretched over the horizon, when a sudden and furious wind broke the open lattice-work of the gallery. The sultana, beside herself, her heart beating, tried to plunge back into the interior of the apartment, but an irresistible power held her where she was, and forced her, against her will, to contemplate the mournful scene before her eyes. A great silence now reigned. Darkness had insensibly covered the earth. Then suddenly a streak of blue light furrowed the clouds in the direction of the pyramids. The princess could distinguish their enormous mass against the horizon as clearly as if it had been noonday. The spectacle thus suddenly revealed, chilled her with fear. Several times did she try to call her slaves, but her voice refused its office. She endeavored to clap her hands, but in vain.

While she remained thus—as if in the grip of some horrible dream—a lamentable voice broke into the stillness, and uttered these words: "My latest breath has just been exhaled into the waters of the river; vainly have thy servants striven to stifle the voice of truth; it rises now from the abysses of death. O wretched mother! see whence issues that fatal light, and tremble!"

Ghulendi Begum endured to hear no more. She fell back senseless. Her women, who had been anxious about her, hurried up at this moment, and uttered the most piercing cries. The Sages approached, and placed into the hands of my father, who was in terrible perturbation, the powerful elixir they had prepared. Scarcely had a few drops fallen on the sultana's breast, when her soul, which had seemed about to follow the orders of Asrael, the Angel of Death, came back, as if in nature's despite, to reanimate her body. Her eyes reopened to see, still illumining the pyramids, the fatal furrow of blue light which had not yet faded from the sky. She raised her arms, and, pointing out to the Émir with her finger that dread portent, was seized with the pains of childbirth, and, in the paroxysm of an unspeakable anguish, brought into the world a son and a daughter: the two wretched beings you see before you here.

The Émir's joy in the possession of a male child was greatly dashed when he saw my mother die before his eyes. Notwithstanding his excessive grief, however, he did not lose his head, and at once handed us over to the care of his Sages. The nurses, who had been engaged in great number, wished to oppose this arrangement; but the ancient men, all uttering incantations simultaneously, compelled them to silence. The cabalistic lavers in which we were to be immersed stood all ready prepared; the mixture of herbs exhaled a vapor that filled the whole palace. Shadan, whose very stomach was turned by the odour of these unspeakable drugs, had all the trouble in the world to restrain himself from summoning the Imans, and doctors of the law, in order to oppose the impious rites now in contemplation. Would to Heaven he had had the courage to do so! Ah, how terrible has been the influence upon us of the pernicious immersions to which we were then subjected! In short, Lord, we were plunged, both successively and together, into a hell-broth which was intended to impart to us a strength and intelligence more than human, but has only instilled into our veins the ardent elixir of a too exquisite sensibility, and the poison of an insatiable desire.

It was to the sound of brazen wands beating against the metal sides of the lavers, it was in the midst of thick fumes issuing from heaps of burning herbs, that invocations were addressed to the Jinns, and specially to those who preside over the pyramids, in order that we might be endowed with miraculous gifts. After this we were delivered over to the nurses, who scarcely could hold us in their arms, such was our liveliness and vivacity. The good women shed tears when they saw how our young blood boiled within us, and strove in vain to cool its effervescence, and to calm us by cleansing our bodies from the reeking mess with which they were still covered; but, alas! the harm was already done! Nay, if even, as sometimes happened in after days, we wished to fall into the ordinary ways of childhood, my father, who was deter-

mined at all hazards to possess children of an extraordinary nature, would brisk us up with heating drugs and
the milk of negresses.

We thus became unendurably headstrong and met-
tlesome. At the age of seven, we could not bear contradiction. At the slightest restraint, we uttered cries of rage,
and bit those who had us in charge till the blood flowed.
Shaban came in for a large share of our attentions in this
kind; sighing over us, however, in silence, for the Émir
only regarded our spitefulness as giving evidence of a
genius equal to that of Saurid and Charobé. Ah! how
little did anyone suspect the real cause of our forward-
ness! Those who look long into the light are soonest
afflicted with blindness. My father had not yet remarked
that we were never arrogant and overbearing towards
one another; that each was ready to yield to the other's
wishes; that Kalilah, my brother, was never at peace save
in my arms; and that, as for me, my only happiness lay in
overwhelming him with caresses.

Up to this time, we had in all things been educated
together: the same book was always placed before the
eyes of both, each turned over the leaves alternately.
Though my brother was subjected to a course of study
rigorous, and above his years, I insisted on sharing it
with him. Abou Taher Achmed, who cared for nothing
save the aggrandisement of his son, gave directions that
in this I should be humored, because he saw that his son
would only fully exert himself when at my side.

We were taught not only the history of the most
remote ages of antiquity, but also the geography of distant lands. The Sages never ceased to indoctrinate us
with the abstruse and ideal moral code, which, as they
pretended, lurked hidden in the hieroglyphics. They
filled our ears with a magnificent verbiage about wisdom
and foreknowledge, and the treasure houses of the Pha-

raohs, whom sometimes they compared to ants, and sometimes to elephants. They inspired us with a most ardent curiosity as to those mountains of hewn stone beneath which the Egyptian kings lie sepulchered. They compelled us to learn by heart the long catalogue of architects and masons who had labored at the building of them. They made us calculate the quality of provisions that would be required by the workmen employed, and how many threads went to every ell of silk with which Sultan Saurid had covered his pyramid. Together with all this rubbish, these most weariful old dotards bewildered our brains with a pitiless grammar of the language spoken of old by the priests in their subterranean labyrinths.

The childish games in which we were allowed to indulge, during our playtime, had no charms for us unless we played them together. The princesses, our sisters, wearied us to death. Vainly did they embroider for my brother the most splendid vests. Kalilah disdained their gifts, and would only consent to bind his lovely hair with the muslin that had floated over the breast of his beloved Zulkaïs. Sometimes they invited us to visit them in the twelve pavilions which my father, no longer hoping to have that number of sons, had abandoned to their use—erecting another, and of greater magnificence, for my brother, and for myself. This latter building, crowned by five domes, and situated in a thick grove, was, every night, the scene of the most splendid revels in the harem. My father would come thither, escorted by his most beautiful slaves—each holding in her hand a candlestick with a white taper. How many times has the light of these tapers, appearing through the trees, caused our hearts to beat in sad anticipation? Everything that broke in upon our solitude was in the highest degree distasteful. To hide among the leafage, and listen to its murmur, seemed to us sweeter far than attending to the sound of the lute and the song of the musicians. But these soft luxurious reveries of ours were highly offensive to my father, he would force us back into the cupolaed saloons, and force us to take part in the common amusements.

Every year the Émir treated us with greater sternness. He did not dare to separate us altogether for fear of the effect upon his son, but tried rather to win him from our languorous dalliance by throwing him more and more into the company of young men of his own age. The game of reeds, so famous among the Arabs, was introduced into the courts of the palace. Kalilah gave himself up to the sport with immense energy; but this was only so as to bring the games to a speedier end, and then fly back to my side. Once reunited we would read together, read of the loves of Jussouf and Zelica, or some other poem that spoke of love—or else, taking advantage of our moments of liberty, we would roam through the labyrinth of corridors looking out upon the Nile, always with our arms intertwined, always with eyes looking into each other's eyes. It was almost impossible to track us in the mazy passages of the palace; and the anxiety we inspired did but add to our happiness.

One evening when we were thus tenderly alone together, and running side by side in childish glee, my father appeared before us and shuddered. "Why," said he to Kalilah, "why are you here and not in the great courtyard, shooting with the bow, of else with the horse-trainers training the horses which are to bear you into battle? Must the sun, as it rises and sets, see you only bloom and fade like a weak narcissus flower? Vainly do the Sages try to move you by the most eloquent discourses, and unveil before your eyes the learned mysteries of an older time; vainly do they tell you of warlike and magnanimous deeds. You are now nearly thirteen, and never have you evinced the smallest ambition to distinguish yourself among your fellow-men. It is not in the lurking haunts of effeminacy that great characters are formed; it is not by reading love poems that men are made fit to govern nations! Princes must act; they must show themselves to the world. Awake! Cease to abuse my patience which has too long allowed you to waste your hours by the side of Zulkaïs. Let her, tender creature that she is, continue to play among her flowers, but do you cease to haunt her company from dawn till eve. I see well enough that it is she who is perverting you."

Having spoken these words, which he emphasized by angry and threatening gestures, Abou Taher Achmed took my brother by the arm, and left me in a very abyss of bitterness. An icy numbness overcame me. Though the sun still shed its fullest rays upon the water, I felt as if it had disappeared below the horizon. Stretched at length upon the ground, I did nothing but kiss the sprays of orange flower that Kalilah had gathered. My sight fell upon the drawings he had traced, and my tears fell in greater abundance. "Alas!" said I, "All is over. Our blissful moments will return no more. Why accuse me of perverting Kalilah? What harm can I do him? How can our happiness offend my father? If it was a crime to be happy, the Sages would surely have given us warning."

My nurse Shamelah found me in this condition of languor and dejection. To dissipate my grief she immediately led me to the grove where the young girls of the harem were playing at hide-and-seek amid the golden aviaries of which the place was full. I derived some little solace from the song of the birds, and the murmur of the rillets of clear water that trickled round the roots of the trees, but when the hour came at which Kalilah was wont to appear these sounds did but add to my sufferings.

Shamelah noticed the heavings of my breast; she drew me aside, placed her hand upon my heart, and observed me attentively. I blushed, I turned pale, and that very visibly. "I see very well," said she, "that it is your brother's absence that so upsets you. This is the fruit of the strange education to which you have been subjected. The holy reading of the Koran, the due observance of the Prophet's laws, confidence in the known mercies of Allah, these are as milk to cool the fever heat of human passion. You know not the soft delight of lifting up your soul to Heaven, and submitting without a murmur to its decrees. The Émir, alas! would forestall the future; while, on the contrary, the future should be passively awaited. Dry your tears; perchance Kalilah is not unhappy though distant from your side."

"Ah!" I cried, interrupting her with a sinister look, "if I were not fully convinced that he is unhappy, I should myself be far more miserable."

Shamelah trembled at hearing me speak thus. She cried: "Would to Heaven that they had listened to my advice, and the advice of Shaban, and instead of handing you over to the capricious teaching of the Sages, had left you, like true believers, at peace in the arms of a blissful and quiet ignorance. The ardour of your feelings alarms me in the very highest degree. Nay, it excites my indignation. Be more calm; abandon your soul to the innocent pleasures that surround you, and do so without troubling yourself whether Kalilah shares in those pleasures or not. His sex is made for toil and manly hardship. How should you be able to follow him in the chase, to handle a bow, and to dart reeds in the Arab game? He must look for companions manly and worthy of himself, and cease to fritter away his best days here at your side amid bowers and aviaries."

This sermon, far from producing its desired effect, made me altogether beside myself. I trembled with rage, and, rising to my feet like one bereft of reason, I rent my veil into ten thousand pieces, and, tearing my breast, cried with a loud voice that my nurse had mishandled me.

The games ceased. Everyone crowded about me; and though the princesses did not love me overmuch, because I was Kalilah's favorite sister, yet my tears, and the blood that flowed from my self-inflicted wounds, excited their indignation against Shamelah. Unfortunately for the poor woman, she had just awarded a severe punishment to two young slaves who had been guilty of stealing pomegranates; and these two little vipers, in order to be revenged, bore testimony against her, and confirmed all I said. They ran, and retailed their lies to my father, who, not having Shaban at his side, and being, moreover, in a good temper because my brother had just thrown a javelin into a crocodile's eye, ordered Shamelah to be tied to a tree, and whipped without mercy.

Her cries pierced my heart. She cried without ceasing: "O you, whom I have carried in my arms, whom I have fed from my breast, how can you cause me to suffer thus? Justify me! Declare the truth! It is only because I tried to save you from the black abyss, into which your wild and unruly desires cannot fail to precipitate you in the end, that you are thus causing this body of mine to be torn to shreds."

I was about to ask that she should be released and spared further punishment, when some demon put into my mind the thought that it was she who, conjointly with Shaban, had inspired my father with the desire of making a hero of Kalilah. Whereupon I armed myself against every feeling of humanity, and cried out that they should go on whipping her till she confessed her crime. Darkness at last put an end to this horrible scene. The victim was unloosed. Her friends, and she had many, endeavored to close her wounds. They asked me, on their knees, to give them a sovereign balm which I possessed, a balm which the Sages had prepared. I refused. Shamelah was placed before my eyes on a litter, and, of set purpose, kept for a moment in front of the place where I stood. That breast, on which I had so often slept, streamed with blood. At this spectacle, at the memory of the tender care she had taken of my infancy, my heart at last was moved—I burst into tears; I kissed the hand she feebly extended to the monster she had nourished in her bosom; I ran to fetch the balm; I applied it myself, begging her, at the same time, to forgive me, and declaring openly that she was innocent, and I alone guilty.

This confession caused a shudder to pass among all who surrounded us. They recoiled from me with horror. Shamelah, though half dead, perceived this, and stifled her groans with the skirt of her garment so as not to add to my despair and the baleful consequences of what I had done. But her efforts were vain. All fled, casting upon me looks that were evil indeed.

The litter was removed, and I found myself alone. The night was very dark. Plaintive sounds seemed to issue from the cypresses that cast their shadows over the place. Seized with terror, I lost myself amid the black foliage, a prey to the most harrowing remorse. Delirium laid its hand upon me. The earth seemed to yawn before my feet, and I to fall headlong into an abyss which had no bottom. My spirit was in this distraught condition when, through the thick underwood, I saw shine the torches of my father's attendants. I noticed that the cortège stopped suddenly. Someone issued from the crowd. A lively presentiment made my heart beat. The footsteps came nearer; and, by the light of a faint and doleful glimmer, such as prevails in the place where we now are, I saw Kalilah appear before me.

"Dear Zulkaïs," cried he, intermingling words and

kisses, "I have passed an age without seeing you, but I have spent it in carrying out my father's wishes. I have fought with one of the most formidable monsters of the river. But what would I not do when, for recompense, I am offered the bliss of spending a whole evening with you alone? Come! Let us enjoy the time to the full. Let us bury ourselves among these trees. Let us, from our retreat, listen, disdainful, to the tumultuous sound of music and dances. I will cause sherbet and cakes to be served on the moss that borders the little porphyry fountain. There I shall enjoy your sweet looks, and charming converse, till the first dawn of the new day. Then, alas! I must plunge once more into the world's vortex, dart accursed reeds, and undergo the interrogatories of Sages."

Kalilah said all this with such volubility that I was unable to put in a word. He drew me after him, scarce resisting. We made our way through the leafage to the fountain. The memory of what Shamelah had said concerning my excessive tenderness for my brother, had, in my own despite, produced a strong impression upon me. I was about to withdraw my hand from his, when, by the light of the little lamps that had been lit on the margin of the fountain, I saw his charming face reflected in the waters, I saw his large eyes dewy with love, I felt his looks pierce to the very bottom of my heart. All my projects of reform, all my agony of remorse, made way for a ferment of very different feelings. I dropped on the ground by Kalilah's side, and leaning his head upon my breast, gave a free course to my tears. Kalilah, when he saw me thus crying passionately, eagerly asked me why I wept. I told him all that had passed between myself and Shamelah, without omitting a single particular. His heart was at first much moved by the picture I drew of her sufferings; but, a moment after, he cried: "Let the officious slave perish! Must the heart's soft yearnings ever meet with opposition! How should we not love one another, Zulkaïs? Nature caused us to be born together. Has not nature, too, implanted in us the same tastes, and a kindred ardour? Have not my father and his Sages made us partakers in the same magic baths? Who could blame a sympathy all has conspired to create? No, Zulkaïs, Shaban and our superstitious nurse may say what they please. There is no crime in our loving one another. The crime would rather be if we allowed ourselves, like cowards, to be separated. Let us swear—not by the Prophet, of whom we have little knowledge, but by the elements that sustain man's existence—let us swear that, rather than consent to live the one without the other, we will take into our veins the soft distillation of the flowers of the stream, which the Sages have so often vaunted in our hearing. That essence will lull us painlessly to sleep in each other's arms, and so bear our souls imperceptibly into the peace of another existence."

These words quieted me. I resumed my ordinary gaiety, and we played and sported together. "I shall be very valiant tomorrow," Kalilah would say, "so as to purchase such moments as these, for it is only by the promise of such a prize that my father can induce me to submit to his fantastic injunctions."

"Ha, ha!" cried Abou Taber Achmed, issuing from behind some bushes, where he had been listening. "Is that your resolve! We will see if you keep to it! You are already fully paid this evening for the little you have done during the day. Hence! And as to you, Zulkaïs, go and weep over the terrible outrage you have committed against Shamelah."

In the greatest consternation we threw ourselves at his feet; but, turning his back upon us, he ordered the eunuchs to conduct us to our separate apartments.

It was no scruple with regard to the kind and quality of our love that exercised the Émir. His sole end was to see his son become a great warrior, and a potent prince, and with regard to the character of the means by which that end was to be obtained, he cared not one tittle. As for me, he regarded me only as an instrument that might have its uses; nor would he have felt any scruples concerning the danger of inflaming our passion by the alternation of obstacles and concessions. On the other hand, he foresaw that indolence and pleasure, too constantly indulged in, must necessarily interfere with his designs. He deemed it necessary, therefore, to adopt with us a harsher and more decided line of conduct than he had hitherto done; and in an unhappy moment he carried that resolution into effect. Alas! without his precautions, his projects, his accursed foresight, we should have remained in innocence, and never been brought to the horror of this place of torment!

The Émir, having retired to his apartments, caused Shaban to be summoned, and imparted to him his fixed resolve to separate us during a certain time. The prudent eunuch prostrated himself immediately, with his face to the ground, and then, rising to his feet, said: "Let my lord forgive his slave if he ventures to be of a different opinion. Do not loose upon this nascent flame the winds of opposition and absence, lest the final conflagration should be such as you are unable to master. You know the Prince's impetuous disposition; his sister has today given proofs, only too signal, of hers. Suffer them to remain together without contradiction; leave them to their childish propensities. They will soon grow tired of one another; and Kalilah, disgusted with the monotony of the harem, will beg you on his knees to remove him from its precincts."

"Have you done talking your nonsense?" interrupted the Emir impatiently. "Ah, how little do you know the genius of Kalilah! I have carefully studied him, I have seen that the operations of my Sages have not been void of their effect. He is incapable of pursuing any object with indifference. If I leave him with Zulkaïs, he will be utterly drowned in effeminacy. If I remove her from him, and make their reunion the price of the great things I require at his hands, there is nothing of which he will not prove himself capable. Let the doctors of our law dote as they please! What can their idle drivel matter so long as he becomes what I desire him to be? Know besides, O eunuch, that when he has once tasted the delights of ambition, the idea of Zulkaïs will evaporate in his mind as a light morning mist absorbed into the rays of the noonday sun—the sun of glory. Therefore enter tomorrow morning into the chamber of Zulkaïs, forestall her awakening, wrap her up in these robes, and convey her, with her slaves and all that may be necessary to make her life pleasant, to the borders of the Nile, where a boat will be ready to receive you. Follow the course of the stream for twenty-nine days. On the thirtieth you will disembark at the Isle of Ostriches. Lodge the princess in the palace which I have had built for the use of the Sages who roam those deserts—deserts replete with ruins and with wisdom. One of these Sages you will find there, called the Palm-tree-climber, because he pursues his course of contemplation upon the tops of the palm-trees. This ancient man knows an infinite number of stories, and it will be his care to divert Zulkaïs, for I know very well that, next to Kalilah, stories are the chief object of her delight."

Shaban knew his master too well to venture upon any further opposition. He went, therefore, to give the necessary orders, but sighed heavily as he went. He had not the slightest desire to undertake a journey to the Isle of Ostriches, and had formed a very unfavorable opinion of the Palm-tree-climber. He was himself a faithful Mussulman, and held the Sages and all their works in abomination.

Everything was made ready all too soon. The agitation of the previous day had greatly fatigued me, so that I slept very heavily. I was taken from my bed so quietly, and carried with such skill, that I never woke till I was at a distance of four leagues from Cairo. Then the noise of the water gurgling round the boat began to alarm me. It filled my ears strangely, and I half fancied I had drunk of the beverage spoken of by Kalilah, and been borne beyond the confines of our planet. I lay thus, bewildered with strange imaginings, and did not dare to open my eyes, but stretched out my arms to feel for Kalilah. I thought he was by my side. Judge of the feelings of hateful surprise to which I was doomed, when, instead of touching his delicate limbs, I seized hold of the horny hand of the eunuch who was steering the boat, and was even older, and more grotesquely ugly, than Shaban himself.

I sat up and uttered piercing cries. I opened my eyes, and saw before me a waste stretch of sky, and of water bounded by bluish banks. The sun was shining in its fullness. The azure heavens caused all nature to rejoice. A thousand river birds played around amid the waterlilies, which the boat shot through at every moment, their large yellow flowers shining like gold, and exhaling a sweet perfume. But all these objects of delight were lost upon me, and, instead of rejoicing my heart, filled me with a somber melancholy.

Looking about me, I saw my slaves in a state of desolation, and Shaban who, with an air at once of discontent and authority, was making them keep silence. The name of Kalilah came at every moment to the tip of my tongue. At last I spoke it aloud, with tears in my eyes, and asked where he was, and what they intended to do with me. Shaban, instead of replying, ordered his eunuchs to re-double their exertions, and to strike up an Egyptian song, and sing in time to the cadence of their oars. Their accursed chorus rang out so potently that it brought an even worse bewilderment in my brain. We shot through the water like an arrow. It was in vain that I begged the rowers to stop, or at least to tell me where I was going. The barbarous wretches were deaf to my entreaties. The more insistent I was, the louder did they roar out their detestable song so as to drown my cries. Shaban, with his cracked voice, made more noise than the rest.

Nothing can express the torments I endured, and the horror I felt at finding myself so far from Kalilah, and on the waters of the fearful Nile. My terrors increased with nightfall. I saw, with an inexpressible anguish, the sun go losing itself in the waters—its light, in a thousand rays, trembling upon their surface. I brought to mind the quiet moments which, at that same hour, I had passed with Kalilah, and, hiding my head in my veil, I gave myself up to despair.

Soon a soft rustling became audible. Our boat was shearing its way through banks of reeds. A great silence succeeded to the song of the rowers, for Shaban had landed. He came back in a few moments, and carried me to a tent, erected a few paces from the river's bank. I found there lights, mattresses stretched on the ground, a table covered with various kinds of food, and an im-mense copy of the Koran, unfolded. I hated the holy book. The Sages, our instructors, had often turned it into ridicule, and I had never read it with Kalilah. So I threw it contemptuously to the ground. Shaban took upon him-self to scold me; but I flew at him, and endeavored to reduce him to silence. In this I proved successful, and the same treatment retained its efficacy during the whole course of the long expedition.

Our subsequent experiences were similar to those of the first day. Endlessly did we pass banks of water-lilies, and flocks of birds, and an infinite number of small boats that came and went with merchandize.

At last we began to leave behind us the plain country. Like all who are unhappy and thus led to look forward, I kept my eyes continually fixed on the horizon ahead of us, and one evening I saw, rising there, great masses of much greater height, and of a form infinitely more varied, than the pyramids. These masses proved to be mountains. Their aspect inspired me with fear. The terrible thought occurred to me that my father was sending me to the woeful land of the Negro king, so that I might be offered up as a sacrifice to the idols, who, as the Sages pretended, were greedy of princesses. Shaban perceived my increasing distress, and at last took pity upon me. He revealed our ultimate destination, adding that though my father wished to separate me from Kalilah, it was not forever, and that, in the meanwhile, I should make the acquaintance of a marvelous personage, called the Palm-tree-climber, who was the best story-teller in the universe.

This information quieted me to some extent. The hope, however distant, of seeing Kalilah again, poured balm into my soul, and I was not sorry to hear that I should have stories to my liking. Moreover, the idea of a realm of solitude, such as the Ostrich Isle, flattered my romantic spirit. If I must be separated from him whom I cherished more than life itself, I preferred to undergo my fate rather in some savage spot than amid the glitter and chatter of a harem. Far from all such impertinent frivolities, I purposed to abandon my whole soul to the sweet memories of the past, and give a free course to the languorous reveries in which I could see again the loved image of my Kalilah.

Fully occupied with these projects, it was with heed-less eyes that I saw our boat approaching nearer and nearer to the land of mountains. The rocks encroached more and more upon the border of the stream, and seemed soon about to deprive us of all sight of the sky. I saw trees of immeasurable height whose intertwisted roots hung down in the water. I heard the noise of cata-racts, and saw the boiling eddies flash in foam and fill the air with a mist thin as silver gauze. Through this veil I perceived, at last, a green island of no great size, on which the ostriches were gravely promenading. Still further forward I discerned a domed edifice standing against a hill all covered with nests. This palace was utterly strange of aspect, and had, in truth, been built by a noted cabalist. The walls were of yellow marble, and shone like polished metal, and every object reflected in them assumed gigantic proportions. I trembled when I saw what fantastic figures the ostriches presented as seen in that strange mirror; their necks seemed to go losing themselves in the clouds, and their eyes shone like enor-mous balls of iron heated red in a furnace.

My terrors were observed by Shaban, who made me understand the magnifying qualities of the palace walls, and assured me that even if the birds were really as mon-strous as they appeared, I might trust, in all security, to their good manners, since the Palm-tree-climber had been laboring for over a hundred years to reduce their disposition to an exemplary mildness. Scarcely had he furnished me with this information, when I landed at a spot where the grass was green and fresh. A thousand unknown flowers, a thousand shells of fantastic shape, a thousand oddly fashioned snails, adorned the shore. The ardour of the sun was tempered by the perpetual dew distilled from the falling waters, whose monotonous sound inclined to slumber.

Feeling drowsy, I ordered a penthouse to be affixed to one of the palm-trees of which the place was full; for the Palm-tree-climber, who always bore at his girdle the keys of the palace, was at that hour pursuing his meditations at the other end of the island.

While a soft drowsiness took possession of my senses, Shaban ran to present my father's letters to the man of wisdom. In order to do this, he was compelled to attach the missives to the end of a long pole, as the Climber was at the top of a palm-tree fifty cubits high, and refused to come down without knowing why he was summoned. So soon as he had perused the leaves of the roll, he carried them respectfully to his forehead, and slipped down like a meteor; and indeed he had somewhat the appearance of a meteor, for his eyes were of flame, and his nose was a beautiful blood-red.

Shaban, amazed by the rapidity of the old man's descent, uninjured, from the tree, was somewhat outraged when asked to take him on his back; but the Climber declared that he never so far condescended as to walk. The eunuch, who loved neither Sages nor their caprices, and regarded both as the plagues of the Émir's family, hesitated for a moment; but, bearing in mind the positive order he had received, he conquered his aversion, and took the Palm-tree-climber on his shoulders, saying: "Alas, the good hermit Abou Gabdolle Guehaman would not have behaved after this manner, and would, moreover, have been much more worthy of my assistance."

The Climber heard these words in high dudgeon, for he had aforetime had pious squabbles with the hermit of the Sandy Desert; so he administered a mighty kick on to the small of Shaban's back, and thrust a fiery nose into the middle of his countenance. Shaban, on this, stumbled, but pursued his way without uttering a syllable.

I was still asleep. Shaban came up to my couch, and, throwing his burden at my feet, said, and his voice had a certain ring in it that woke me without difficulty: "Here is the Climber! Much good may he do you!"

At the sight of such an object, I was quite unable, notwithstanding all my sorrows, to help bursting out into a fit of uncontrollable laughter. The old man did not change countenance, notwithstanding; he jingled his keys with an air of importance, and said to Shaban, in grave tones: "Take me again upon your back; let us go to the palace, and I will open its doors, which have never, hitherto, admitted any member of the female sex save my great egg-layer, the queen of the ostriches."

I followed. It was late. The great birds were coming down from the hills, and surrounded us in flocks, pecking at the grass and at the trees. The noise they made with their beaks was such that I seemed to be listening to the feet of an army on the march. At last I found myself before the shining walls of the palace. Though I knew the trick of them, my own distorted figure terrified me, as did also the figure of the Climber on the shoulders of Shaban.

We entered into a vaulted apartment, lined with black marble starred with golden stars, which inspired a certain feeling of awe—a feeling to which, however, the old man's grotesque and amusing grimaces afforded some relief. The air was stifling and nearly made me sick. The Climber, perceiving this, caused a great fire to be lit, and threw into it a small aromatic ball which he drew from his bosom. Immediately a vapor, rather pleasant to the smell, but very penetrating, diffused itself throughout the room. The eunuch fled, sneezing. As for me, I drew near the fire, and sadly stirring the ashes, began to form in them the cipher of Kalilah.

The Climber did not interfere. He praised the education I had received, and approved greatly of our immersions, just after birth, by the Sages, adding maliciously that nothing so sharpened the wits as a passion somewhat out of the common. "I see clearly," he continued, "that you are absorbed in reflections of an interesting nature; and I am well pleased that it should be so. I myself had five sisters; we made very light of Mahomet's teachings, and loved each other with some fervor. I still, after the lapse of a hundred years, bear this in my memory with pleasure, for we scarcely ever forget early impressions. Thus my constancy has greatly commended me to the Jinns whose favorite I am. If you are able, like myself, to persevere in your present sentiments, they will probably do something for you. In the meanwhile, place your confidence in me. I shall not prove surly or unsympathetic as a guardian and keeper. Don't get it into your head that I am dependent on the caprice of your father, who has a limited outlook, and prefers ambition to pleasure. I am happier amid my palms, and my ostriches, and in the enjoyments of the delights of meditation, than he in his divan, and in all his grandeur. I don't mean to say that you yourself cannot add to the pleasures of my life. The more gracious you are to me, the more shall I show civility to you, and make you the partaker in things of beauty. If you seem to be happy in this place of solitude, you will acquire a great reputation for wisdom, and I know, by my own experience, that under the cloak of a great reputation it is possible to hide whole treasures of folly. Your father in his letters has told me all your story. While people think that you are giving heed to my instructions, you can talk to me about your Kalilah as much as you like, and without offending me in anyway. On the contrary, nothing affords me greater pleasure than to observe the movements of a heart abandoning itself to its youthful inclinations, and I shall be glad to see the bright colors of a first love mantling on young cheeks."

While listening to this strange discourse, I kept my eyes on the ground, but the bird of hope fluttered in my bosom. At last I looked at the Sage, and his great red nose, that shone like a luminous point in that room of black marble, seemed to me less disagreeable. The smile accompanying my glance was of such significance that the Climber easily perceived I had swallowed his bait. This pleased him so mightily that he forgot his learned indolence, and ran to prepare a repast of which I stood greatly in need.

Scarcely had he departed, when Shaban came in, holding in his hand a letter, sealed with my father's seal, which he had just opened. "Here," said he, "are the instructions I was only to read when I reached this place; and I have read them only too clearly. Alas! how wretched it is to be the slave of a prince whose head has been turned by much learning! Unhappy princess! I am compelled, much against my will, to abandon you here. I must re-embark with all who have followed me hither, and only leave in your service the lame Mouzaka, who is deaf and dumb. The wretched Climber will be your only helper. Heaven alone knows what you will gain from his companionship. The Émir regards him as a prodigy of learning and wisdom; but as to this he must suffer a faithful Mussulman to have his doubts." As he spoke these words, Shaban touched the letter three times with his forehead, and then, leaping backwards, disappeared from my sight.

The hideous manner in which the poor eunuch wept on leaving me, amused me much. I was far indeed from making any attempt to keep him back. His presence was odious to me, for he always avoided all conversation about the only subject that filled my heart. On the other hand, I was enchanted at the choice of Mouzaka as my attendant. With a deaf and dumb slave, I should enjoy full liberty in imparting my confidences to the obliging old man, and in following his advice, if so be that he gave me advice of which I approved.

All my thoughts were thus assuming a somewhat rosy hue, when the Climber returned, smothered up in carpets and cushions of silk, which he stretched out on the ground; and he then proceeded, with a pleasant and contented air, to light torches, and to burn pastilles in braziers of gold. He had taken these sumptuous articles from the palace treasury, which, as he assured me, was well worthy of exciting my curiosity. I told him I was quite ready to take his word for it at that particular time, the smell of the excellent viands which had preceded him having very agreeably whetted my appetite. These viands consisted chiefly of slices of deer spiced with fragrant herbs, of eggs prepared after divers recipes, and of cakes more dainty and delicate than the petals of a white rose. There was besides a ruddy liquor, made of date juice, and served in strange translucent shells, and sparkling like the eyes of the Climber himself.

We lay down to our meal together in very friendly fashion. My amazing keeper greatly praised the quality of his wine, and made very good use of it, to the intense surprise of Mouzaka, who, huddled up in a corner, indulged in undescribable gestures which the marble reflected on all sides. The fire burnt gaily, throwing out sparks, which, as they darkened, exhaled an exquisite perfume. The torches gave a brilliant light, the braziers shone brightly, and the soft warmth that reigned in the apartment inclined to a voluptuous indolence.

The situation in which I found myself was so singular, the kind of prison in which I was confined was so different from anything I could have imagined, and the ways of my keeper were so grotesque, that from time to time I rubbed my eyes to make sure that the whole thing was not a dream. I should even have derived amusement from my surroundings, if the thought that I was so far from Kalilah had left me for a single moment. The Climber, to distract my thoughts. began the marvelous story of the Giant Gebri, and the artful Charodé, but I interrupted him, and asked him to listen to the recital of my own real sorrows, promising that, afterwards, I should give ear to his tales. Alas! I never kept that promise. Vainly, at repeated intervals, did he try to excite my curiosity: I had none save with regard to Kalilah, and did not cease to repeat: "Where is he? What is he doing? When shall I see him again?"

The old man, seeing me so headstrong in my passion, and so well resolved to brave all remorse, became convinced that I was a fit object for his nefarious purposes, for, as my hearers will doubtless have already understood, he was a servant of the monarch who reigns in this place of torment. In the perversity of his soul, and that fatal blindness which makes men desire to find an entrance here, he had vowed to induce twenty wretches to serve Eblis, and he exactly wanted my brother and myself to complete that number. Far indeed was he, therefore, from really trying to stifle the yearnings of my heart; and though, in order to fan the flame that consumed me, he seemed from time to time, to be desirous of telling me stories, yet, in reality, his head was filled with quite other thoughts.

I spent a great part of the night in making my criminal avowals. Towards morning I fell asleep. The Climber did the same, at a few paces' distance, having first, without ceremony, applied to my forehead a kiss that burned me like a red-hot iron. My dreams were of the saddest.

They left but a confused impression on my mind; but, so far as I can recollect, they conveyed the warnings of Heaven, which still desired to open before me a door of escape and of safety.

So soon as the sun had risen, the Climber led me into his woods, introduced me to his ostriches, and gave me an exhibition of his supernatural agility. Not only did he climb to the tremulous tops of the tallest and most slender palms, bending them beneath his feet like ears of corn, but he would dart like an arrow from one tree to another. After the display of several of these gymnastic feats, he settled on a branch, told me he was about to indulge in his daily meditations, and advised me to go with Mouzaka and bathe by the border of the stream, on the other side of the hill.

The heat was excessive. I found the clear waters cool and delicious. Bathing-pools, lined with precious marbles, had been hollowed out in the middle of a little level mead over which high rocks cast their shadow. Pale narcissi and gladioli grew on the margin, and, leaning towards the water, waved over my head. I loved these languid flowers, they seemed an emblem of my fortunes, and for several hours I allowed their perfumes to intoxicate my soul.

On returning to the palace, I found that the Climber had made great preparations for my entertainment. The evening passed like the evening before; and from day to day, pretty nearly after the same manner, I spent four months. Nor can I say that the time passed unhappily. The romantic solitude, the old man's patient attention, and the complacency with which he listened to love's foolish repetitions, all seemed to unite in soothing my pain. I should perhaps have spent whole years in merely nursing those sweet illusions that are so rarely realized, have seen the ardour of my passion dwindle and die, have become no more than the tender sister and friend of Kalilah, if my father had not, in pursuit of his wild schemes, delivered me over to the impious scoundrel who sat daily watching at my side to make me his prey. Ah! Shaban! ah, Shamelah! you, my real friends, why was I torn from your arms? Why did you not, from the very first, perceive the germs of a too passionate tenderness existing in our hearts, germs which ought then and there to have been extirpated, since the day would come when not fire and steel would be of any avail!

One morning when I was steeped in sad thoughts, and expressing in even more violent language than usual my despair at being separated from Kalilah, the old man fixed upon me his piercing eyes, and addressed me in these words: "Princess, you, who have been taught by the most enlightened of Sages, cannot doubtless be ignorant of the fact that there are Intelligences, superior to the race of man, who take part in human affairs, and are able to extricate us from the greatest difficulties. I, who am telling you this, have had experience, more than once, of their power; for I had a right to their assistance, having been placed, as you yourself have been, under their protection from birth. I quite see that you cannot live without your Kalilah. It is time, therefore, that you should apply for aid to such helpful spirits. But will you have the strength of mind, the courage to endure the approach of Beings so different from mankind? I know that their coming produces certain inevitable effects, as internal tremors, the revulsion of the blood from its ordinary course; but I know also that these terrors, these revulsions, painful as they undoubtedly are, must appear as nothing compared with the mortal pain of separation from an object loved greatly and exclusively. If you resolve to invoke the Jinn of the Great Pyramid, who, as I know, presided at your birth, if you are willing to abandon yourself to his care, I can, this very evening, give you speech of your brother, who is nearer than you imagine. The Being in question, so renowned among the Sages, is called Omoultakos: he is, at present, in charge of the treasure which the ancient cabalist kings have placed in this desert. By means of the other spirits under his command, he is in close touch with his sister, whom, by the by, he loved in his time just as you now love Kalilah. He will, therefore, enter into your sorrows just as much as I do myself, and will, I make no doubt, do all he can to further your desires."

At these last words, my heart beat with unspeakable violence. The possibility of seeing Kalilah once again excited a transport in my breast. I rose hastily, and ran about the room like a mad creature. Then, coming back to the old man's side, I embraced him, called him my father, and throwing myself at his knees, I implored him, with clasped hands, not to defer my happiness, but to conduct me, at whatever hazard, to the sanctuary of Omoultakos.

The crafty old scoundrel was well pleased, and saw with a malicious eye into what a state of delirium he had thrown me. His only thought was how to fan the flame thus kindled. For this purpose, he resumed a cold and reserved aspect, and said, in tones of great solemnity: "Be it known to you, Zulkaïs, that I have my doubts, and cannot help hesitating, in a matter of such importance, great as is my desire to serve you. You evidently do not know how dangerous is the step you propose to take; or, at least, you do not fully appreciate its extreme rashness. I cannot tell how far you will be able to endure the fearful solitude of the immeasurable vaults you must traverse, and the strange magnificence of the place to which I must conduct you. Neither can I tell in what shape the Jinn will appear. I have often seen him in a form so fearful that my senses have long remained numbed; at other times he has shown himself under an aspect so grotesque that I have scarcely been able to refrain from choking laughter, for nothing can be more capricious than beings of that nature. Omoultakos, mayhap, will spare your weakness; but it is right to warn you that the adventure on which you are bound is perilous, that the moment of the Jinn's apparition is uncertain, that while you are waiting in expectation you must show neither fear nor horror, nor impatience, and that, at the sight of him, you must be very sure not to laugh, and not to cry. Observe, moreover, that you must wait in silence, and the stillness of death, and with your hands crossed over your breast, until he speaks to you, for a gesture, a smile, a groan, would involve not only your destruction, but also that of Kalilah, and my own."

"All that you tell me," I replied, "carries terror into my bosom; but, impelled by such a fatal love as mine, what would one not venture!"

"I congratulate you on your sublime perseverance," rejoined the Climber, with a smile of which I did not then appreciate the full significance and wickedness. "Prepare yourself. As soon as darkness covers the earth, I will go and suspend Mouzaka from the top of one of my highest palm-trees, so that she may not be in our way. I will then lead you to the door of the gallery that leads to the retreat of Omoultakos. There I shall leave you, and myself, according to my custom, go and meditate at the top of one of the trees, and make vows for the success of your enterprise."

I spent the interval in anxiety and trepidation. I wandered aimlessly amid the valleys and hillocks on the island. I gazed fixedly into the depths of the waters. I watched the rays of the sun declining over their surface, and looked forward, half in fear and half in hope, to the moment when the light should abandon our hemisphere.

The holy calm of a serene night at last overspread the world.

I saw the Climber detach himself from a flock of ostriches that were gravely marching to drink at the river. He came to me with measured steps. Putting his finger to his lips, he said: "Follow me in silence."

I obeyed. He opened a door, and made me enter, with him, into a narrow passage, not more than four feet high, so that I was compelled to walk half doubled up. The air I breathed was damp and stifling. At every step I caught my feet in viscous plants that issued from certain cracks and crevices in the gallery. Through these cracks the feeble light of the moon's rays found an entrance, shedding light, every here and there, upon little wells that had been dug to right and left of our path. Through the black waters in these wells I seemed to see reptiles with human faces.

I turned away my eyes in horror. I burned with desire to ask the Climber what all this might mean, but the gloom and solemnity of his looks made me keep silence. He appeared to progress painfully, and to be brushing aside with his hands something to me invisible. Soon I was no longer able to see him at all. We were going, as it seemed, round and round in complete darkness; and, so as not to lose him altogether in that frightful labyrinth, I was compelled to lay hold upon his robe.

At last we reached a place where I began to breathe a freer and fresher air. A solitary taper of enormous size, fixed upright in a block of marble, lighted up a vast hall, and discovered to my eyes five staircases, whose banisters, made of different metals, faded upwards into the darkness. There we stopped, and the old man broke the silence, saying: "Chose between these staircases. One only leads to the treasury of Omoultakos. From the others, which go losing themselves to cavernous depths, you would never return. Where they lead you would find nothing but hunger, and the bones of those whom famine has aforetime destroyed."

Having said these words, he disappeared, and I heard a door closing behind him.

Judge of my terror, you who have heard the ebony portals, which confine us forever in this place of torment, grind upon their ebony hinges! Indeed, I dare to say that my position was, if possible, even more terrible than yours, for I was alone. I fell to the earth at the base of the block of marble. A sleep, such as that which ends our mortal existence, overcame my senses. Suddenly a voice, clear, sweet, insinuating like the voice of Kalilah, flattered my ears. I seemed, as in a dream, to see him on the staircase, the banisters of which were of brass. A majestic warrior, whose pale front bore a diadem, held him by the hand. "Zulkaïs," said Kalilah, with an afflicted air, "Allah forbids our union. But Eblis, whom you see here, extends to us his protection. Implore his aid, and follow the path to which he points you."

I awoke in a transport of courage and resolution, seized the taper, and began, without hesitation, to ascend the stairway with the brazen banisters. The steps seemed to multiply beneath my feet; but my resolution never faltered; and, at last, I reached a chamber, square, and immensely spacious, and paved with a marble that was of flesh color, and marked as with the veins and arteries of the human body. The walls of this place of terror were hidden by huge piles of carpets of a thousand kinds, and a thousand hues, and these moved slowly to and fro, as if painfully stirred by human creatures stifling beneath their weight. All around were ranged black chests, whose steel padlocks seemed encrusted with blood. Muffled hissings appeared to issue from under the lids of some of these chests; from others, groans and cries as of indistinct voices, and metallic clinkings. I thought that the voices were those of dives, or afrits, rather than men. I shuddered, and fled on, all the more precipitately because some of them had seemed to call me by name. The chamber was endless, and I saw that I had been mistaken as to its form. It enlarged itself before me, like the perspectives of a hall of ill dreams. Insensibly, and as if by the operation of some enchantment, it assumed a more frightful aspect. The marble pavement was now of that livid color seen in the flesh of bodies after death, its veinings were dark as if blood had coagulated within them, and were interspersed with mottlings such as would be made on human skin by the contusions of iron maces. Columns, higher than the monumental pillars of the old kings of Egypt, rose round me into gloom that the great taper was unable to pierce. A blue mist, such as might ascend from nether gulfs, wavered like a curtain before the removed walls, and the light flickered woefully in my arms, as it met the dank sighing exhaled by the subterranean reaches.

I had need of all my resolution, and was forced to summon up the loved image of Kalilah, with all possible clearness, before I could proceed any further. The vastness of the room, its dismal character and furnishings, terrified me more and more. A weakness seized upon my limbs and senses, the taper became an almost insupportable burden, and I could scarce uplift it to inspect the curious treasures piled about me. Notwithstanding this, I perceived that there were open caskets, overrunning with divers jewels, with goldwork wrought in the fashion of antiquity, and still untarnished; so that I felt sure, at first, that I had reached the treasury of Omoultakos, the Jinn to whom the cabalist kings had entrusted their wealth. But soon doubt came upon me, as I began to note the hideous confusion that prevailed everywhere, the human finger-bones, and other charnel relics, that were heaped without discrimination amid the precious stones, or stored in separate vessels of graven silver, as if they too had been of rare worth. I saw, also, that some of the larger caskets were really sarcophagi, such as were used by the Egyptians. They had been brimmed with skulls, and the severed members of mummies, and gold coins. Serpents, milk-white, and wholly scaleless, crept to and fro, bringing in their mouths bright jewels, or fragments of bone, which they deposited in certain receptacles that were not yet filled to the rim.

A faintness, such as the dying must undergo, would have overcome me at the sight of these horrors, and the musty odours which they emitted; but I was revived by an extraordinary apparition, which, through the speed and brilliance of its descent from one of the topless pillars, I took for a moment to be the Palm-tree-climber. The apparition reached the floor in a flash; it rose up, and I saw my mistake. It was almost more than I could do to refrain from bursting into wild laughter, for the uncommon personage before me resembled, as much as anything else, a mangy baboon whose hair had fallen out in broad patches. His head and face, indeed, were altogether hairless, like those of the ancient priests, but the brows had been painted with kohl to relieve their blank appearance, and the same cosmetic had been applied in large mouches about the jowls. He carried at his side, from a girdle of human gut, a capacious and somewhat tattered pouch, in the form of a stomach sac, from whose rifts unmentionable objects protruded. More amazing than all this, however, was the long tail, seeming to be on fire perpetually, which the remarkable being flourished in my face like a torch.

Recalling the injunctions of the Climber, I succeeded in smothering my mirth, and maintained a strict silence.

It was well, no doubt, that I did so. Omoultakos, for it was indeed the Jinn himself, addressed me in a hollow and lugubrious voice that accorded somewhat strangely with his aspect, saying: "Princess, you need carry no longer the immense taper whose weight has grown so burdensome to you. My tail, which burns with inexhaustible fire, will now serve as a flambeau for us both."

He indicated a half-empty sarcophagus, in which, with expressive signs, he told me to deposit the taper, leaving it upright, so that the grease would not gutter upon the rare contents of that reliquary. Then he said to me: "As a fitting reward for your perseverance in daring the shadows of the subterranean labyrinth, I shall show you the many treasures which have been amassed in this chamber, during the eras of my custodianship. To the wealth of the cabalist rulers, in itself quite prodigious, I have since added much that I prize peculiarly. Eblis, it is true, in his deep-lying halls, has been able to gather together a far more inclusive assortment of terrestrial riches; but I venture to assert that my collection, in some ways, is a little choicer than his. For example, in this casket, you behold, among other remnants of former delight and beauty, a thigh-bone that once belonged to Balkis."

He waved his tail, which flared brightly, above the relic in question, and then, with a ludicrous and proprietary air, passed on to others. At one time, during our tour, he paused before a small box of green bronze, filled with a dark brown powder, and lifting a pinch of the powder to his nostrils, gave vent to prolonged and violent sternutations. When these had ceased, he remarked with much satisfaction: "There is, to my knowledge, no sneezing-powder more efficacious than the one I have just employed, which was obtained through the atomizing of the mummies of antique embalmers."

My astonishment and disgust were mingled with a strange propensity to laughter, which I conquered again and yet again, with much difficulty. Omoultakos, in a most extensive circuit of inspection about the chamber, illumined for me with the unfailing light of his appendage, an infinite variety of objects that testified to mortal corruption. All the while, he discoursed upon their quondam ownership, and their history, in a fashion that was no less proud than funereal. He showed me, moreover, certain musical instruments, which he himself had designed during hours of leisure. Among them, I remember that there were lutes fashioned from the ribs and arm-bones of women, and stringed with male sinews, and also there were tabors of human skin, that had a deep sonority. On more than one of these instruments, he played a while for my diversion, and though I thought the airs he extorted from them were more than atrocious, I felt that it would be politic to commend, rather than criticize, his playing. In the meanwhile, I burned with desire to question him regarding the whereabouts of Kalilah, and the means through which we might again be united; but mindful of all that the Climber had told me, I restrained my eagerness.

At last, Omoultakos, who had led me on for a great distance between the columns, and the sarcophagi, and had laid aside his unusual instruments of music, turned on me, and said: "Think not, O princess, that all my treasures are things which have come down from antiquity. In the recesses of this unfathomable chamber, objects of more recent date are also conserved. One of them, at least, will interest you. Be patient, and follow the illumination of my tail."

With this adjuration, he conducted me to an open sarcophagus, gilded, and carved from end to end with hieroglyphics, that stood a little apart from the others. In it, with unutterable horror and anguish, I discerned the form of Kalilah, lying as if dead, with a mortal pallor on his cheeks, and lips, and eyelids. I noted that the bosom of his raiment was torn and bloody. I hurled myself upon him, and sought to revive him with kisses, but in vain.

Omoultakos, at this point, chose to interrupt my efforts by inserting the agile tip of his combustive tail between myself and the face of Kalilah. He observed, in a severe tone: "There is but one way in which the prince, your beloved brother, can be revived. The method, fortunately, lies at my immediate disposal. First, however, I will explain to you the presence of Kalilah in this place. The Émir Abou Taher Achmed, in attempting to continue the heroic education he designed for your brother, sent him forth with a small retinue the other day, to hunt the ferocious lions of the Nubian Desert. These lions, appearing in unwonted number, and with more than their usual rapacity, disposed of the followers of Kalilah, and would have served the prince in like manner, if some of my subordinate Jinns, who were watching over the expedition, had not intervened. Unluckily, they were too late to keep Kalilah from being wounded almost to death by the talons of the beasts. They brought him here, only a few hours since, and I have permitted him to occupy the sarcophagus of an elder Pharaoh, though my wisdom has told me that the tenancy will be of brief duration, and that Kalilah can not be numbered among my permanent acquisitions. If you, Zulkaïs, will consent to a very simple matter, I will give into your hand, without delay, a supremely sovereign restorative."

"Anything! Anything!" I cried, wildly. "I consent to whatever you ask, if only Kalilah be brought back to life.

"You need promise only one thing," quoth Omoultakos. "Pledge your fealty to Eblis, the lord of the fiery globe, and the shadowy caverns."

"It is pledged," I replied, hastily. "Give me the re-storative."

Omoulkatos, with his apish fingers, began to fumble in the tattered pouch that hung at his girdle. I caught sight of certain highly nauseating oddments, from among which, presently, he produced a pale yellow fruit, having somewhat the form and size of a peach, and laid it in the palm of my hand.

"This fruit," he informed me, "was grown in a garden which, without ever having beheld the sun, is more fertile than the gardens of Irem. If you squeeze it very gently above the lips of Kalilah, a single drop of its juice, falling down upon them, will suffice to resuscitate him in all the bloom that you have loved so dearly. The fruit, after that, is yours to retain; but I trust that you will not be so careless as to devour it at any future time. If you were to do this, the results would be very surprising, since the action of the juice on those who languish at the gates of death, and those who exult in the fulness of life, is an altogether different thing."

Scarcely heeding any of his words, I hastened to squeeze the yellow fruit above Kalilah's lips, which were white as those of a cadaver. I was transported with joy when a living ruby returned into them beneath the dripping of the fluid, and the eyes of Kalilah opened, to give back my ardent gaze. He lifted his arms from the sarcophagus to embrace me, and I quite forgot the presence of Omoultakos. That personage, after a decorous interval, observed in a loud voice: "I am sorry to break in upon your reunion, since I cannot do otherwise than approve and admire the fervor which animates you, but it is more than probable that I shall have, before long, another use for the receptacle you are both occupying. For that reason, I shall conduct you to an alcove beyond my treasury. This alcove is fitted with comfortable couches that will serve your purpose fully as well."

Kalilah, rearing his head at the sound of Omoultakos' voice, perceived, for the first time, the remarkable baboon, who had hitherto been screened from his view by my bosom. He, in his turn, was no less amazed than I had been. However, heeding the injunction of our host, he got up from the sarcophagus. In low tones, I begged him to repress the injudicious laughter that quivered visibly upon his countenance. We both followed Omoultakos. As we went, I placed the yellow fruit in the bosom of my garment.

Kalilah, more impressed by the person of our guide than by the doleful surroundings, could not forbear commenting on the igneous properties of the tail, which emitted showers of sparks on the gloom, as the owner flourished it in his progress. He remarked to me, in great wonder, that the baboon seemed to experience no discomfort whatever from this unique process of combustion. Omoultakos, who had overheard him, turned and said: "Know, young prince, that it is the nature of my tail to burn in this manner, and the sensation it affords me is, in its degree, no more painful, or extraordinary, than that which women experience from the flushing of their cheeks, or men from an excitement of the blood."

After a journey that appeared brief indeed, and which I could not reconcile with my former impression of the vastness of the chamber, we came to an open portal. The flambeau of Omoultakos, reared aloft, illumined for us a much smaller room, with couches of golden cloth, and dark draperies. My father would have loved the draperies, since they were entirely covered with hieroglyphics; but the hieroglyphics, which appeared to change altogether from moment to moment, would have maddened the Sages whom he employed. Here the Jinn left us, after lighting with his torch the many lamps of brass, and copper censers, with which the room had been supplied. I thought that this departure was attended by an odd lack of ceremony, but recalled that he had come down from the pillar, on the occasion of his appearance before me, in a manner no less informal. Through the open doorway, Kalilah and I continued, for some time, to see the luminosity that he made in his movements about the treasury. He seemed to be very busy, and we caught glimpses of certain peculiar assistants, who were bringing in a new lot of treasures. But our joy in being together once more, preoccupied us so fully, that we paid little heed to these activities, and were enabled to disregard, for the time being, their somewhat sinister import.

Between our caresses, we asked each other a thousand questions, and told all that had happened to us severally, since the date of our separation. Kalilah was much dismayed when he learned the circumstances of my visit to the underground palace, and the promise I had made, on his behalf, to the Jinn. "Alas!" he said, "I fear that all this has been prearranged, and for no good purpose. The lions who attacked me were of supernatural size and fierceness. No doubt they were the very Jinns of whom Omoultakos told you, and after their talons had slain my followers, and had rendered me senseless, they brought me here. You, Zulkaïs, through your affection for me, have entered the trap. However, let us try to forget this. No matter how dark and precarious our situation, we have at least the consolation of each other's society."

"All that I have done was nothing," I replied. "Gladly would I pledge myself to Eblis a thousand times, for your sake."

In such converse, the hours went by, and we began to wonder at the long absence of Omoultakos, who had vanished after a while among the pillars of the treasury, and had not returned. He had left us without declaring his intentions as to our future destiny, and it seemed that he had forgotten us. Moreover, he had made no provision for us, beyond lighting the lamps and censers. By the illumination that these vessels yielded, we began to remark the moth-holes in the figured hangings, and the great age of the couches, whose coverings might have been exhumed from palaces long buried in the desert sand. We noted, also, that the lamps and censers were overspread with verdigris. The fumes of the latter vessels troubled us, being both musty and aromatic, like the balms that exhale from the cerements of the Pharaohs. We heard, at intervals, equivocal and disquieting sounds, in a direction of which we were not sure. Together with all this, I grew faint with hunger, but there were no viands in the room for my regalement. At last, I remembered the fruit which I had placed in my bosom, after using it to revive Kalilah. Forgetful of the warning of the Jinn, I drew it forth. I would have shared it with Kalilah, but he, noting my hunger, declined. I devoured it greedily, finding a strange and spicy savor in its pulp.

Almost immediately, I experienced a feeling of unbearable heat, an intense ardour of life rose within me, as if it would burst the confines of my heart. The chamber seemed to blaze with a light that was not that of the lamps. My senses burned with a confused delirium of desires, a madness possessed me, and Kalilah was lost to my perception, like the shadows of the apartment. Then I thought that a ball of fire, hued with a thousand colors that changed momently, swam up and floated before me in the air. An extravagant longing seized me, to possess the ball, and I sprang to my feet and tried to clasp it, but the globe eluded me, and fled swiftly, and I, without heeding the cries of Kalilah, pursued it. I ran through a small portal at the rear of the chamber, and down a labyrinth of cavernous corridors, which, save for the illumination of the globe, would have been altogether lightless. Intent only on overtaking the bright ball, I did not notice my surroundings, or the route I followed. At last, the light disappeared, leaving only a dim glimmer, like the afterglow of the sunken sun, and I came to the verge of a precipice. Far below, the ball receded, plunging into abysses from which the dismal and eternal roaring of lost waters came up to arrest me. However, in my delirium, I should still have followed the globe, if it had not seemed, after an interval, to return toward me from the depths. I waited, ready to seize it, but, as the light drew nearer, I perceived its true source. It was Omoultakos, climbing nimbly from the gulf, by means of the slight projections of the stone.

In an instant, he stood beside me, and said, with an air of reproof: "Princess, why this haste to fling yourself into the underground river that flows eternally toward the realms of Eblis? The destined hour of your departure thither, borne by that doleful tide, is not yet at hand. Fortunately, I met your brother, who was seeking you in the darkness of the caverns; and, learning what had happened, I came without delay, by another route than yours, to intercept you. Kalilah, in consideration of this act of succor, has plighted himself to the prince of the fiery globe, and the flaming hearts. Let us rejoin him, for I fear that he still wanders, lost and distracted, in the darkness. In a sense, I am to blame for what has occurred. Carried away by the duties of my custodianship of the treasury—duties that are often exigent—I forgot the obligations of a host, and failed to provide for your natural needs. If I had done as I should, hunger would never have prompted you to devour the fruit that gave rise to your delirium."

My madness had abated. I followed Omoultakos,

perceiving, as I went, the horrors of the labyrinth of caverns, to which the orb with the thousand colors had blinded me. At every turn, there were scattered bones, and skeletons, which had belonged, mayhap, to wretches who had lost themselves in the maze, and had perished of famine. Some of the skeletons lay close together, but I could not tell whether the intimacy of their postures had been dictated by human love, or anthropophagism. Omoultakos did not enlighten me upon this point, nor did I care to question him. At last, we found Kalilah, whose joy was little less extravagant than the delirium which had led me to the floating ball.

"I must provide more adequately for your entertainment," said Omoultakos. "Eblis permits me to keep you here a while, as my guests. My subterranean garden lies not far away, and in it is a pavilion, which you may occupy. Food and drink will be served regularly to you, and in plenteous quantities, and I trust that neither of you will be tempted, in view of what has occurred, to sample the fruit of my trees."

He conducted us along a short passage, from which we emerged into an immense cavern whose roof was purple like the vault of night, and was starred with effulgent ores that resembled the planets and the constellations. Here we beheld the garden of which he had spoken. It consisted of fantastic trees, heavily laden with divers fruits and blossoms and cunningly illumed by lamps, which, very often, I could not distinguish from the fruits. In the midst was a small pavilion, built of a marble mottled with rose and black. It was furnished with luxurious divans, and a table on which delicious viands, and wines like molten ruby and topaz, had been spread for our refection. Omoultakos, after again assuring us of his hospitality, begged leave to excuse himself, and departed with the same celerity that had marked his former movements.

In the pavilion he had placed at our disposal, Kalilah and I dwelt for a period of time that neither of us could calculate. That period, however, in spite of certain forebodings, was the happiest we had known, since our childhood days when the Émir was still content to leave us together without interruption. In that place, there was no difference between day and night: for the lamps burned eternally amid the fruited foliage, and the starlike ores continued to sparkle ever in the vault above us. Often we wandered through the garden, which had a strange beauty, though we did not care, after certain indiscreet delvings, to examine too closely into its hidden particulars. The odours of the blossoms, richer than myrrh and santal, conduced to an agreeable languor; and since the Jinn supplied us with an infinity of savorous foods, and wines more delicate than those of Persia, we were well content to leave his fruits alone. In the happiness of being together, and in transports renewed perpetually, we almost forgot the rash pledges we had given. Nor were we troubled overmuch by the fact that the attendants who served us were invisible, and gave proof of their presence only by a sound that resembled the noise made by the flittering of great bats. Also, for the most part, we found ourselves able to ignore a sullen roaring that pervaded the garden continually, seeming to issue from subterranean waters, at a vague distance, and in a direction of which we were never sure. Indeed, we became so accustomed to the sound, mournful and menacing though it was, that it seemed to us little more than a quality of the silence in which we were sequestered.

Our host, who was no doubt busily engaged with the care of his acquisitions, and the treasure confided to him by the cabalist rulers, failed to visit us again. We remarked his negligence, but under the circumstances, we did not miss him.

Alas! though we knew it not, or strove to forget it, the malign forces of our destiny were always at work. Our sojourn in the garden of Omoultakos was to have a frightful denouement. By virtue of the allegiance we had both pledged to the Lord of Evil, we were to share, at the appointed time, the fate of all others who have thus damned themselves irretrievably. And yet—in order to live again those happy hours—I, and Kalilah, too, would repeat the same bond without hesitation. Dream not that we repent.

We were plighting other vows, as we had done a thousand times, and were seated upon a divan in the pavilion, when the date of perdition arrived. It came without announcement, save an insupportable thunder, that seemed to rive apart the foundations of the world. We were tossed as if by earthquake, the air darkened around us, and the ground gave way. Clasped in each other's arms, we had the sensation of falling, together with the pavilion, into a deep abyss. The thunder ceased, the vertigo of our descent grew less, and we heard on every side the woeful and furious noise of rushing waters. A melancholy glimmering dawned about us, and by it, we saw the pavilion had become a raft of serpents plaited together in the fashion of reeds, that was borne headlong on a dark tumultuous river. The serpents, large and rigid as beams of wood, had preserved on their skins the black and rosy mottling of the marble, and they had formed themselves into a cabin around us, like the superstructure of the pavilion. As we went, they added a loud and sinister hissing to the sound of the driven waters.

In this horrible manner, we were carried through unfathomable caves, ever deeper, toward the accursed realms of Eblis. Night surrounded us, we beheld no longer the least ray or glimmer, and, clasped tightly in each other's embrace, we sought by means of such contact to mitigate the noisome clamminess of the reptiles, and the terror of our situation. Thus we seemed to go on for a length of time that was equivalent to many days.

At last, a light broke upon us, lurid and doleful, and the clamor of the river deepened, with a thunder of mighty waterfalls before us. We thought surely that the torrent would precipitate us over some fatal verge, but at this point, the serpents of our raft began to exert themselves, and swimming vigorously, they landed us in the halls of Eblis, not far from that place where the Sultan Soliman listens eternally to the tumult of the cataract, and waits for the release that will come to him only with its cessation. After that, preserving no longer the form of a raft, they reentered the stream, and swam back separately, in the direction of the garden of Omoultakos. Now, lord, we await, even as you, the moment when our hearts shall be kindled with the unconsuming fire, and shall burn brightly as the tail of the baboon—but, alas! shall derive unutterable anguish, like the hearts of all other mortals, from that flame in which is the ecstasy of demons.

THIRTEEN PHANTASMS

have been faithful to thee, Cynara, in my fashion."

John Alvington tried to raise himself on the pillow as he murmured in his thoughts the long-familiar refrain of Dowson's lyric. But his head and shoulders fell back in an overflooding helplessness, and there trickled through his brain, like a thread of icy water, the realization that perhaps the doctor had been right — perhaps the end was indeed imminent. He thought briefly of embalming fluids, immortelles, coffin nails and falling sods; but such ideas were quite alien to his trend of mind, and he preferred to think of Elspeth. He dismissed his mortuary musings with an appropriate shudder.

He often thought of Elspeth, these days. But of course he had never really forgotten her at any time. Many people called him a rake; but he knew, and had always known, that they were wrong. It was said that he had broken, or materially dented, the hearts of twelve women, including those of his two wives; and strangely enough, in view of the exaggerations commonly characteristic of gossip, the number was correct. Yet he, John Alvington, knew to a certainty that only one woman, who no one reckoned among the twelve, had ever really mattered in his life.

He had loved Elspeth and no one else; he had lost her through a boyish quarrel which was never made up, and she had died a year later. The other women were all mistakes, mirages: they had attracted him only because he fancied, for varying periods, that he had found in them something of Elspeth. He had been cruel to them perhaps, and most certainly he had not been faithful. But in forsaking them, had he not been all the truer to Elspeth?

Somehow his mental image of her was more distinct

today than in years. As if a gathering dust had been wiped away from a portrait, he saw with strange clearness the elfin teasing of her eyes and the light tossing of brown curls that always accompanied her puckish laughter. She was tall — unexpectedly tall for so fairylike a person, but all the more admirable thereby; and he had never liked any but tall women.

How often he had been startled, as if by a ghost, in meeting some women with a similar mannerism, a similar figure or expression of eyes or cadence of voice; and how complete had been his disillusionment when he came to see the unreality and fallaciousness of the resemblance. How irreparably she, the true love, had come sooner or later between him and all the others.

He began to recall things that he had almost forgotten, such as the carnelian cameo brooch she had worn on the day of their first meeting, and a tiny mole on her left shoulder, of which he had once had a glimpse when she was wearing a dress unusually low-necked for that period. He remembered too the plain gown of pale green that clung so deliciously to her slender form on that morning when he had flung away with a curt good-bye, never to see her again. . . .

Never, he thought to himself, had his memory been so good: surely the doctor was mistaken, for there was no failing of his faculties. It was quite impossible that he should be mortally ill, when he could summon all his recollections of Elspeth with such ease and clarity.

Now he went over all the days of their seven months' engagement, which might have ended in a felicitous marriage if it had not been for her propensity to take unreasonable offense, and for his own answering flash of temper and want of conciliatory tactics in the crucial quarrel. How near, how poignant it all seemed. He wondered what malign providence had ordered their parting and had sent him on a vain quest from face to illusory face for the remainder of his life.

He did not, could not remember the other women — only that he had somehow dreamed for a little while that they resembled Elspeth. Others might consider him a Don Juan: but he knew himself for a hopeless sentimentalist, if there ever had been one.

What was that sound? he wondered. Had someone opened the door of the room? It must be the nurse, for no one else ever came at that hour in the evening. The nurse was a nice girl, though not at all like Elspeth. He tried to turn a little so that he could see her, and somehow succeeded, by a titanic effort altogether disproportionate to the feeble movement.

It was not the nurse after all, for she was always dressed in immaculate white befitting her profession. This woman wore a dress of cool, delectable green, pale as the green of shoaling sea-water. He could not see her face, for she stood with back turned to the bed; but there was something oddly familiar in that dress, something that he could not quite remember at first. Then, with a distinct shock, he knew that it resembled the dress worn by Elspeth on the day of their quarrel, the same dress he had been picturing to himself a little while before. No one ever wore a gown of that length and style nowadays. Who on earth could it be? There was a queer familiarity about her figure, too, for she was quite tall and slender.

The woman turned, and John Alvington saw that it was Elspeth — the very Elspeth from whom he had parted with a bitter farewell, and who had died without ever permitting him to see her again. Yet how could it be but Elspeth, when she had been dead so long? Then, by a swift transition of logic, how could she have ever died, since she was here before him now? It seemed so infinitely preferable to believe that she still lived, and he wanted so much to speak to her, but his voice failed him when he tried to utter her name.

Now he thought that he heard the door open again, and became aware that another woman stood in the shadows behind Elspeth. She came forward, and he observed that she wore a green dress identical in every detail with that worn by his beloved. She lifted her head — and the face was that of Elspeth, with the same teasing eyes and whimsical mouth! But how could there be two Elspeths?

In profound bewilderment, he tried to accustom himself to the bizarre idea; and even as he wrestled with a problem so unaccountable, a third figure in pale green, followed by a fourth and a fifth came in and stood beside the first two. Nor were these the last, for others entered one by one, till the room was filled with women, all of whom wore the raiment and the semblance of his dead sweetheart. None of them uttered a word, but all looked at Alvington with a gaze in which he now seemed to discern a deeper mockery than the elfin tantalizing he had once found in the eyes of Elspeth.

He lay very still, fighting with a dark, terrible perplexity. How could there be such a multitude of Elspeths, when he could remember knowing only one? And how many were there, anyway? Something prompted him to count them, and he found that there were thirteen of the specters in green. And having ascertained this fact, he was struck by something familiar about the number. Didn't people say that he had broken the hearts of thirteen women? Or was the total only twelve? Anyway, if you counted Elspeth herself, who had really broken his heart, there would be thirteen.

Now all the woman began to toss their curly heads, in a manner he recalled so well, and all of them laughed with a light and puckish laughter. Could they be laughing at him? Elspeth had often done that but he had loved her devotedly nevertheless. . . .

All at once, he began to feel uncertain about the precise number of figures that filled his room; it seemed to him at one moment that there were more than he had counted, and then that there were fewer. He wondered which one among them was the true Elspeth, for after all he felt sure that there had never been a second — only a series of women apparently resembling her, who were not really like her at all when you came to know them.

Finally, as he tried to count them and scrutinize the thronging faces, all of them grew dim and confused and indistinct, and he half forgot what he was trying to do. Which one was Elspeth? Or had there ever been a real Elspeth? He was not sure of anything at the last, when oblivion came, and he passed to that realm in which there are neither women nor phantoms nor love nor numerical problems.

THE RESURRECTION
OF THE RATTLESNAKE

No, as I've told you fellows before, I haven't a red cent's worth of faith in the supernatural."

The speaker was Arthur Avilton, whose tales of the ghostly and macabre had often been compared to Poe, Bierce and Machen. He was a master of imaginative horrors, with a command of diabolically convincing details, of monstrous cobweb suggestions that had often laid a singular spell on the minds of readers who were not ordinarily attracted or impressed by literature of that type. It was his own boast, often made, that all his effects were secured in a purely ratiocinative, even scientific manner, by playing on the element of subconscious dread, the ancestral superstition latent in most human beings; but he claimed that be himself was utterly incredulous of anything occult or fantasmal, and that he had never in his life known the slightest tremor of fear concerning such things.

Avilton's listeners looked at him a little questioningly. They were John Godfrey, a young landscape painter, and Emil Schuler, a rich dilettante, who played in alternation with literature and music, but was not serious in his attentions to either. Both were old friends and admirers of Avilton, at whose house on Sutter Street, in San Francisco, they had met by chance that afternoon. Avilton had suspended work on a new story to chat with them and smoke a sociable pipe. He still sat at his writing-table, with a pile of neatly written foolscap before him. His appearance was as normal and non-eccentric as his handwiriting, and he might have been a lawyer or doctor or chemist, rather than a concocter of bizarre fiction. The room, his library, was quite luxurious, in a sober, gentlemanly sort of fashion, and there was little of the outré in its furnishings. The only unusual notes were struck by two heavy brass candlesticks on his table wrought in the form of rearing serpents, and a stuffed rattlesnake that was coiled on top of one of the low bookcases.

"Well," observed Godfrey, "if anything could convince me of the reality of the supernatural, it would be some of your stories, Avilton. I always read them by broad daylight — I wouldn't do it after dark on a bet . . . By the way, what's the yarn you are working on now?"

"It's about a stuffed serpent that suddenly comes to life," replied Avilton. "I'm calling it *The Resurrection of the Rattlesnake*. I got the idea while I was looking at my rattler this morning."

"And I suppose you'll sit here by candlelight tonight," put in Schuler, "and go on with your cheerful little horror without turning a hair." It was well known that Avilton did much of his writing at night.

Avilton smiled. "Darkness always helps me to concentrate. And, considering that so much of the action in my tales is nocturnal, the time is not inappropriate."

"You're welcome," said Schuler, in a jocular tone. He arose to go, and Godfrey also found that it was time to depart.

"Oh, by the way," said their host, "I'm planning a little weekend party. Would you fellows care to come over next Saturday evening? There'll be two or three others of our friends. I'll have this story off my chest by then, and we'll raise the roof."

Godfrey and Schuler accepted the invitation, and went out together. Since they both lived across the bay, in Oakland, and both were on their way home, they caught the same car to the ferry.

"Old Avilton is certainly a case of the living contradiction, if there ever was one," remarked Schuler. "Of course, no one quite believes in the occult or the necromantic nowadays; but anyone who can cook up such infernally realistic horrors, such thoroughgoing hair-frizzlers as he does, simply hasn't the right to be so cold-blooded about it. I claim that it's really indecent."

"I agree," rejoined his companion. "He's so damnably matter-of-fact that he arouses in me a sort of Hallowe'en impulse: I want to dress up in an old sheet and play ghost or something, just to jar him out of that skeptical complacency of his."

"Ye gods and little ghosties!" cried Schuler. "I've got an inspiration. Remember what Avilton told us about the new story he's writing — about the serpent that comes to life?"

He unfolded the prankish idea he had conceived, and the two laughed like mischievous schoolboys plotting some novel deviltry.

"'Why not? It should give the old lad a real thrill," chuckled Godfrey. "And he'll think that his fictions are more scientific than he ever dreamed before."

"I know where I can get one," said Schuler. "I'll put it in a fishing-creel, and hide the creel in my valise next Saturday when we go to Avilton's. Then we can watch our chance to make the substitution."

On Saturday evening the two friends arrived together at Avilton's house, and were admitted by a Japanese who combined in himself the roles of cook, butler, housekeeper and valet. The other guests, two young musicians, had already come, and Avilton, who was evidently in a mood for relaxation, was telling them a story, which, to judge from the continual interruptions of laughter, was not at all in the vein for which he had grown so famous. It seemed almost impossible to believe that he could be the author of the gruesome and brain-freezing horrors that bore his name.

The evening went successfully, with a good dinner, cards, and some pre-war Bourbon, and it was after midnight when Avilton saw his guests to their chambers, and sought his own.

Godfrey and Schuler did not go to bed, but sat up talking in the room they occupied together, till the house had grown silent and it was probable that everyone had fallen asleep. Avilton, they knew, was a sound sleeper, who boasted that even a rivet factory or a brass orchestra could not keep him awake for five minutes after his head had touched the pillow.

"Now's our chance," whispered Schuler, at last. He had taken from his valise a fishing-creel, in which was a large and somewhat restless gopher-snake, and softly opening the door, which they had left ajar, the conspirators tiptoed down the hall toward Avilton's library, which lay at the farther end. It was their plan to leave the live gopher-snake in the library in lieu of the stuffed rattler, which they would remove. A gopher-snake is somewhat similar to a rattler in its markings; and, in order to complete the verisimilitude, Schuler had even provided himself with a set of rattlers, which he meant to attach with thread to the serpent's tail before freeing it. The substiution, they felt, would undoubtedly prove a trifle startling, even to a person of such boiler-plate nerves and unrelenting skepticism as Avilton.

As if to facilitate their scheme, the door of the library stood half open. Godfrey produced a flashlight, and they entered. Somehow, in spite of their merry mood, in spite of the schoolboy hoax they had planned and the Bourbon they had drunk, the shadow of something dim and sinister and disquieting fell on the two men as they crossed the threshold. It was like a premonition of some unknown and unexpected menace, lurking in the darkness of the book-peopled room where Avilton had woven so many of his weird and spectral webs. They both began to remember incidents of nocturnal horror from his stories — happenings that were ghoulishly hideous or necromantically strange and terrible. Now, such things seemed even more plausible than the author's diabolic art had made them heretofore. But neither of the men could have quite defined the feeling that came over them or could have assigned a reason for it.

"I feel a little creepy," confided Schuler, as they stood in the dark library. "Turn on that flashlight, won't you?"

The light fell directly on the low bookcase where the stuffed rattler had been coiled, but to their surprise, they found the serpent missing from its customary place.

"Where is the damned thing, anyway?" muttered Godfrey. He turned his light on the neighboring bookcases, and then on the floor and chairs in front of them, but without revealing the object of his search. At last, in its circlings, the ray struck Avilton's writing-table, and they saw the snake, which, in some mood of grotesque humor, Avilton had evidently placed on his pile of manuscript to serve in lieu of a paperweight. Behind it gleamed the two serpentine candlesticks.

"Ah! there you are," said Schuler. He was about to open his creel when a singular and quite unforeseen thing occurred. He and Godfrey both saw a movement on the writing-table, and before their incredulous eyes the rattlesnake coiled on the pile of paper slowly raised its arrow-shaped head and darted forth its forky tongue! Its cold, unwinking eyes, with a fixation of baleful intensity well-nigh hypnotic, were upon the intruders, and as they stared in unbelieving horror, they heard the sharp rattling of its tail, like withered seeds in a wind-swung pod.

"My God!" exclaimed Schuler. "The thing is alive!"

As he spoke, the flashlight fell from Godfrey's hand and went out, leaving them in soot-black darkness. As they stood for a moment, half petrified with astonishment and terror, they heard the rattling again, and then the sound of some object that seemed to strike the floor in falling. Once more, in a few instants, there came the sharp rattle, this time almost at their very feet.

Godfrey screamed aloud, and Schuler began to curse incoherently, as they both turned and ran toward the open door. Schuler was ahead, and as he crossed the threshold into the dim-lit hall, where one electric bulb still burned, he heard the crash of his companion's fall, mingled with a cry of such infinite terror, such atrocious agony, that his brain and his very marrow were turned to ice. In the paralyzing panic that overtook him, Schuler retained no faculty except that of locomotion, and it did not even occur to him that it would be possible to stop and ascertain what had befallen Godfrey. He had no thought, no desire, except to put the length of the hall between himself and that accursed library and its happenings.

Avilton, dressed in pajamas, stood at the door of his room. He had been aroused by Godfrey's scream of terror.

"What's the matter?" the story-writer queried, with a look of amiable surprise, which turned to a real gravity when he saw Schuler's face. Schuler was as white as a marble headstone and his eyes were preternaturally dilated.

"The snake!" Schuler gasped. "The snake! The snake! Something awful has happened to Godfrey — he fell with the thing just behind him."

"What snake? You don't mean my stuffed rattler by any chance, do you?"

"Stuffed rattler?" yelled Schuler. "The damned thing is alive! It came crawling after us, rattling under our very

feet a moment ago. Then Godfrey stumbled and fell —
and he didn't get up."

"I don't understand," purred Avilton. "The thing is a
manifest impossibility — really quite contrary to all natural laws, I assure you. I killed that snake four years ago,
in El Dorado County, and had it stuffed by an expert taxi-
dermist."

"Go and see for yourself," challenged Schuler.

Avilton strode immediately to the library and turned
on the lights. Schuler, mastering a little his panic and his
dreadful forebodings, followed at a cautious distance. He
found Avilton stooping over the body of Godfrey, who
lay quite still in a huddled and horribly contorted position near the door. Not far away was the abandoned
fishing-creel. The stuffed rattlesnake was coiled in its
customary place on top of the bookshelves.

Avilton, with a grave and brooding mien, removed
his hand from Godfrey's heart, and observed:

"He's quite dead — shock and heart failure, I should
think."

Neither he nor Schuler could bear to look very long
at Godfrey's upturned face, on which was stamped — as
with some awful brand or acid an expression of fear and
suffering beyond all human capacity to endure. In their
mutual desire to avoid the lidless horror of his dead
staring, their eyes fell at the same instant on his right
hand, which was clenched in a hideous rigidity and
drawn close to his side.

Neither could utter a word when they saw the thing
that protruded from between Godfrey's fingers. It was a
bunch of rattles, and on the endmost one, where it had
evidently been torn from the viper's tail, there clung several shreds of raw and bloody flesh.

THE NAMELESS OFFSPRING

*Many and multiform are the dim horrors of Earth, infesting
her ways from the prime. They sleep beneath the unturned stone;
they rise with the tree from its roots; they move beneath the sea and
in subterranean places; they dwell in the inmost adyta; they emerge
betimes from the shutten sepulcher of haughty bronze and the low
grave that is sealed with clay. There be some that are long known to
man, and others as yet unknown that abide the terrible latter days
of their revealing. Those which are the most dreadful and the
loathliest of all are haply still to be declared. But among those that
have revealed themselves aforetime and have made manifest their
veritable presence, there is one which may not openly be named for
its exceeding foulness. It is that spawn which the hidden dweller in
the vaults has begotten upon mortality.*

— From the *Necronomicon* of Abdul Alhazred

In a sense, it is fortunate that the story I must now relate
should be so largely a thing of undetermined shadows,
of half-shaped hints and forbidden inferences. Otherwise, it could never be written by human hand or read by
human eye. My own slight part in the hideous drama
was limited to its last act; and to me its earlier scenes were
merely a remote and ghastly legend. Yet, even so, the broken reflex of its unnatural horrors has crowded out in
perspective the main events of normal life; has made
them seem no more than frail gossamers, woven on the
dark, windy verge of some unsealed abyss, some deep,
half-open charnel, wherein Earth's nethermost corrup-
tions lurk and fester.

The legend of which I speak was familiar to me from
childhood, as a theme of family whispers and head shak-
ings, for Sir John Tremoth had been a schoolmate of my
father. But I had never met Sir John, had never visited

Tremoth Hall, till the time of those happenings which formed the final tragedy. My father had taken me from England to Canada when I was a small infant; he had prospered in Manitoba as an apiarist; and after his death the bee ranch had kept me too busy for years to execute a long-cherished dream of visiting my natal land and exploring its rural byways.

When, finally, I set sail, the story was pretty dim in my memory; and Tremoth Hall was no conscious part of my itinerary when I began a motorcycle tour of the English counties. In any case, I should never have been drawn to the neighborhood out of morbid curiosity, such as the frightful tale might possibly have evoked in others. My visit, as it happened, was purely accidental. I had forgotten the exact location of the place, and did not even dream that I was in its vicinity. If I had known, it seems to me that I should have turned aside, in spite of the circumstances that impelled me to seek shelter, rather than intrude upon the almost demoniacal misery of its owner.

When I came to Tremoth Hall, I had ridden all day, in early autumn, through a rolling countryside with leisurely, winding thoroughfares and lanes. The day had been fair, with skies of pale azure above noble parks that were tinged with the first amber and crimson of the following year. But toward the middle of the afternoon, a mist had come in from the hidden ocean across low hills and had closed me about with its moving phantom circle. Somehow, in that deceptive fog, I managed to lose my way, to miss the mile-post that would have given me my direction to the town where I had planned to spend the ensuing night.

I went on for a while, at random, thinking that I should soon reach another crossroad. The way that I followed was little more than a rough lane and was singularly deserted. The fog had darkened and drawn closer, obliterating all horizons; but from what I could see of it, the country was one of heath and boulders, with no sign of cultivation. I topped a level ridge and went down a long, monotonous slope as the mist continued to thicken with twilight. I thought that I was riding toward the west; but before me, in the wan dusk, there was no faintest gleaming or flare of color to betoken the drowned sunset. A dank odour that was touched with salt, like the smell of sea marshes, came to meet me.

The road turned at a sharp angle, and I seemed to be riding between downs and marshland. The night gathered with an almost unnatural quickness, as if in haste to overtake me; and I began to feel a sort of dim concern and alarm, as if I had gone astray in regions that were more dubious than an English county. The fog and twilight seemed to withhold a silent landscape of chill, deathly, disquieting mystery.

Then, to the left of my road and a little before me, I saw a light that somehow suggested a mournful and tear-dimmed eye. It shone among blurred, uncertain masses that were like trees from a ghostland wood. A nearer mass, as I approached it, was resolved into a small lodge-building, such as would guard the entrance of some estate. It was dark and apparently unoccupied. Pausing and peering, I saw the outlines of a wrought-iron gate in a hedge of untrimmed yew.

It all had a desolate and forbidding air; and I felt in my very marrow the brooding chillness that had come in from the unseen marsh in that dismal, ever-coiling fog. But the light was promise of human nearness on the lonely downs; and I might obtain shelter for the night, or at least find someone who could direct me to a town or inn.

Somewhat to my surprise, the gate was unlocked. It swung inward with a rusty grating sound, as if it had not been opened for a long time; and pushing my motorcycle before me, I followed a weed-grown drive toward the light. The rambling mass of a large manor-house disclosed itself, among trees and shrubs whose artificial forms, like the hedge of ragged yew, were assuming a wilder grotesquery than they had received from the hand of the topiary.

The fog had turned into a bleak drizzle. Almost groping in the gloom, I found a dark door, at some distance from the window that gave forth the solitary light. In response to my thrice-repeated knock, I heard at length the muffled sound of slow, dragging footfalls. The door was opened with a gradualness that seemed to indicate caution or reluctance, and I saw before me an old man, bearing a lighted taper in his hand. His fingers trembled with palsy or decrepitude, and monstrous shadows flickered behind him in a dim hallway, and touched his wrinkled features as with the flitting of ominous, batlike wings.

"What do you wish, sir?" he asked. The voice, though quavering and hesitant, was far from churlish and did not suggest the attitude of suspicion and downright inhospitality which I had begun to apprehend. However, I sensed a sort of irresolution or dubiety; and as the old man listened to my account of the circumstances that had led me to knock at that lonely door, I saw that he was scrutinizing me with a keenness that belied my first impression of extreme senility.

"I knew you were a stranger in these parts," he commented, when I had finished. "But might I inquire your name, sir?"

"I am Henry Chaldane."

"Are you not the son of Mr. Arthur Chaldane?"

Somewhat mystified, I admitted the ascribed paternity.

"You resemble your father, sir. Mr. Chaldane and Sir John Tremoth were great friends, in the days before your father went to Canada. Will you not come in, sir? This is Tremoth Hall. Sir John has not been in the habit of receiving guests for a long time; but I shall tell him that you are here; and it may be that he will wish to see you."

Startled, and not altogether agreeably surprised at the discovery of my whereabouts, I followed the old man to a book-lined study whose furnishings bore evidence of luxury and neglect. Here he lit an oil lamp of antique fashion, with a dusty, painted shade, and left me alone with the dustier volumes and furniture.

I felt a queer embarrassment, a sense of actual intrusion, as I waited in the wan yellow lamplight. There came back to me the details of the strange, horrific, half-forgotten story I had overheard from my father in childhood years.

Lady Agatha Tremoth, Sir John's wife, in the first year of their marriage, had become the victim of cataleptic seizures. The third seizure had apparently terminated in death, for she did not revive after the usual interval, and displayed all the familiar marks of the rigor mortis. Lady Agatha's body was placed in the family vaults, which were of almost fabulous age and extent, and had been excavated in the hill behind the manorhouse. On the day following the interment, Sir John, troubled by a queer, insistent doubt as to the finality of the medical verdict, had reentered the vaults in time to hear a wild cry, and had found Lady Agatha sitting up in her coffin. The nailed lid was lying on the stone floor, and it seemed impossible that it could have been removed by the struggles of the frail woman. However, there was no other plausible explanation, though Lady Agatha herself could throw little light on the circumstances of her strange resurrection.

Half dazed, and almost delirious, in a state of dire terror that was easily understandable, she told an incoherent tale of her experience. She did not seem to remember struggling to free herself from the coffin, but was troubled mainly by recollections of a pale, hideous, unhuman face which she had seen in the gloom on awakening from her prolonged and deathlike sleep. It was the sight of this face, stooping over her as she lay in the open coffin, that had caused her to cry out so wildly. The thing had vanished before Sir John's approach, fleeing swiftly to the inner vaults; and she had formed only a vague idea of its bodily appearance. She thought, however, that it was large and white, and ran like an animal on all fours, though its limbs were semihuman.

Of course, her tale was regarded as a sort of dream, or a figment of delirium induced by the awful shock of her experience, which had blotted out all recollection of its true terror. But the memory of the horrible face and figure had seemed to obsess her permanently, and was plainly fraught with associations of mind-unhinging fear. She did not recover from her illness, but lived on in a shattered condition of brain, and body; and nine months later she died, after giving birth to her first child.

Her death was a merciful thing; for the child, it seemed, was one of those appalling monsters that sometimes appear in human families. The exact nature of its abnormality was not known, though frightful and divergent rumors had purported to emanate from the doctor, nurses and servants who had seen it. Some of the latter had left Tremoth Hall and had refused to return, after a single glimpse of the monstrosity.

After Lady Agatha's death, Sir John had withdrawn from society; and little or nothing was divulged in regard to his doings or the fate of the horrible infant. People said, however, that the child was kept in a locked room with iron-barred windows, which no one but Sir John himself ever entered. The tragedy had blighted his whole life, and he had become a recluse, living alone with one or two faithful servants, and allowing his estate to decline grievously through neglect. Doubtless, I thought, the old man who had admitted me was one of the remaining servitors. I was still reviewing the dreadful legend, still striving to recollect certain particulars that had almost passed from memory, when I heard the sound of footsteps which, from their slowness and feebleness, I took to be those of the returning manservant.

However, I was mistaken; for the person who entered was plainly Sir John Tremoth himself. The tall, slightly bent figure, the face that was lined as if by the trickling of some corrosive acid, were marked with a dignity that seemed to triumph over the double ravages of mortal sorrow and illness. Somehow — though I could have calculated his real age — I had expected an old man; but he was scarcely beyond middle life. His cadaverous pallor and feeble tottering walk were those of a man who is stricken with some fatal malady. His manner, as he addressed me, was impeccably courteous and even gracious. But the voice was that of one to whom the ordinary relations and actions of life had long since become meaningless and perfunctory.

"Harper tells me that you are the son of my old school friend, Arthur Chaldane," he said. "I bid you welcome to such poor hospitality as I am able to offer. I have not received guests for many years, and I fear you will find the Hall pretty dull and dismal and will think me an indifferent host. Nevertheless, you must remain, at least for the night. Harper has gone to prepare dinner for us."

"You are very kind," I replied. "I fear, however, that I am intruding. If — "

"Not at all," he countered firmly. "You must be my

guest. It is miles to the nearest inn, and the fog is chang-
ing into a heavy rain. Indeed, I am glad to have you. You
must tell me all about your father and yourself at dinner.
In the meanwhile, I'll try to find a room for you, if you'll
come with me."

He led me to the second floor of the manor-house
and down a long hall with beams and panels of ancient
oak. We passed several doors which were doubtless
those of bed-chambers. All were closed, and one of the
doors was reenforced with iron bars, heavy and sinister
as those of a dungeon cell. Inevitably I surmised that this
was the chamber in which the monstrous child had been
confined, and also I wondered if the abnormality still
lived, after a lapse of time that must have been nearly
thirty years. How abysmal, how abhorrent, must have
been its departure from the human type, to necessitate an
immediate removal from the sight of others! And what
characteristics of its further development could have
rendered necessary the massive bars on an oaken door
which, by itself, was strong enough to have resisted the
assaults of any common man or beast?

Without even glancing at the door, my host went on,
carrying a taper that scarcely shook in his feeble fingers.
My curious reflections, as I followed him, were interrupted with nerve-shattering suddenness by a loud cry
that seemed to issue from the barred room. The sound
was a long, ever-mounting ululation, infra-bass at first
like the tomb-muffled voice of a demon, and rising
through abominable degrees to a shrill, ravenous fury, as
if the demon had emerged by a series of underground
steps to the open air. It was neither human nor bestial, it
was wholly preternatural, hellish, macabre; and I shuddered with an insupportable eeriness, that still persisted
when the demon voice, after reaching its culmination,
had returned by reverse degrees to a profound sepul-

chral silence.

Sir John had given no apparent heed to the awful sound, but had gone on with no more than his usual faltering. He had reached the end of the hall, and was pausing before the second chamber from the one with the sealed door.

"I'll let you have this room," he said. "It's just beyond the one that I occupy." He did not turn his face toward me as he spoke; and his voice was unnaturally toneless and restrained. I realized with another shudder that the chamber he had indicated as his own was adjacent to the room from which the frightful ululation had appeared to issue.

The chamber to which he now admitted me had manifestly not been used for years. The air was chill, stagnant, unwholesome, with an all-pervading mustiness; and the antique furniture had gathered the inevitable increment of dust and cobwebs. Sir John began to apologize.

"I didn't realize the condition of the room," he said. "I'll send Harper after dinner, to do a little dusting and clearing, and put fresh linen on the bed."

I protested, rather vaguely, that there was no need for him to apologize. The unhuman loneliness and decay of the old manor-house, its lustrums and decades of neglect, and the corresponding desolation of its owner, had impressed me more painfully than ever. And I dared not speculate overmuch concerning the ghastly secret of the barred chamber, and the hellish howling that still echoed in my shaken nerves. Already I regretted the singular fortuity that had drawn me to that place of evil and festering shadows. I felt an urgent desire to leave, to continue my journey even in the face of the bleak autumnal rain and windblown darkness. But I could think of no excuse that would be sufficiently tangible and valid.

Manifestly, there was nothing to do but remain.

Our dinner was served in a dismal but stately room, by the old man whom Sir John had referred to as Harper. The meal was plain but substantial and well-cooked; and the service was impeccable. I had begun to infer that Harper was the only servant — a combination of valet, butler, housekeeper and chef.

In spite of my hunger, and the pains taken by my host to make me feel at ease, the meal was a solemn and almost funereal ceremony. I could not forget my father's story; and still less could I forget the sealed door and the baleful ululation. Whatever it was, the monstrosity still lived; and I felt a complex mingling of admiration, pity and horror as I looked at the gaunt and gallant face of Sir John Tremoth, and reflected upon the lifelong hell to which he had been condemned, and the apparent forti-tude with which he had borne its unthinkable ordeals. A bottle of excellent sherry was brought in. Over this, we sat for an hour or more. Sir John spoke at some length concerning my father, of whose death he had not previ-ously heard; and he drew me out in regard to my own affairs with the subtle adroitness of a polished man of the world. He said little about himself, and not even by hint or implication did he refer to the tragic history which I have outlined.

Since I am rather abstemious, and did not empty my glass with much frequency, the major part of the heavy wine was consumed by my host. Toward the end, it seemed to bring out in him a curious vein of confidenti-ality; and he spoke for the first time of the ill health that was all too patent in his appearance. I learned that he was subject to that most painful form of heart disease, angina pectoris, and had recently recovered from an attack of unusual severity.

"The next one will finish me," he said. "And it may

come at any time — perhaps tonight." He made the announcement very simply, as if he were voicing a commonplace or venturing a prediction about the weather. Then, after a slight pause, he went on, with more emphasis and weightiness of tone:

"Maybe you'll think me queer, but I have a fixed prejudice against burial or vault interment. I want my remains to be thoroughly cremated, and have left careful directions to that end. Harper will see to it that they are fulfilled. Fire is the cleanest and purest of the elements, and it cuts short all the damnable processes between death and ultimate disintegration. I can't bear the idea of some mouldy, worm-infested tomb."

He continued to discourse on the subject for some time, with a singular elaboration and tenseness of manner that showed it to be a familiar theme of thought, if not an actual obsession. It seemed to possess a morbid fascination for him; and there was a painful light in his hollow, haunted eyes, and a touch of rigidly subdued hysteria in his voice, as he spoke. I remembered the interment of Lady Agatha, and her tragic resurrection, and the dim, delirious horror of the vaults that had formed an inexplicable and vaguely disturbing part of her story. It was not hard to understand Sir John's aversion to burial; but I was far from suspecting the full terror and ghastliness on which his repugnance had been founded.

Harper had disappeared after bringing the sherry; and I surmised that he had been given orders for the renovation of my room. We had now drained our last glasses; and my host had ended his peroration. The wind, which had animated him briefly, seemed to die out, and he looked more ill and haggard than ever. Pleading my own fatigue, I expressed a wish to retire; and he, with his invariable courtliness, insisted on seeing me to my chamber and making sure of my comfort, before seeking his own bed.

In the hall above, we met Harper, who was just descending from a flight of stairs that must have led to an attic or third floor. He was carrying a heavy iron pan, in which a few scraps of meat remained; and I caught an odour of pronounced gaminess, almost virtual putrescence, from the pan as he went by. I wondered if he had been feeding the unknown monstrosity, and if perhaps its food were supplied to it through a trap in the ceiling of the barred room. The surmise was reasonable enough, but the odour of the scraps, by a train of remote, half-literary association, had begun to suggest other surmises which, it would seem, were beyond the realm of possibility and reason. Certain evasive, incoherent hints appeared to point themselves suddenly to an atrocious and abhorrent whole. With imperfect success, I assured myself that the thing I had fancied was incredible to science; was a mere creation of superstitious diablerie. No, it could not be . . . here in England, of all places . . . that corpse-devouring demon of Oriental tales and legends . . . the *ghoul*.

Contrary to my fears, there was no repetition of the fiendish howling as we passed the secret room. But I thought that I heard a measured crunching, such as a large animal would make in devouring its food.

My room, though still drear and dismal enough, had been cleared of its accumulated dust and matted gossamers. After a personal inspection, Sir John left me and retired to his own chamber. I was struck by his deathly pallor and weakness, as he said good night to me, and felt guiltily apprehensive that the strain of receiving and entertaining a guest might have aggravated the dire disease from which he suffered. I seemed to detect actual pain and torment beneath his careful armour of urbanity, and wondered if the urbanity had not been maintained at an excessive cost.

The fatigue of my day-long journey, together with the heavy wine I had drunk, should have conduced to early slumber. But though I lay with tightly closed lids in the darkness, I could not dismiss those evil shadows, those black and charnel larvae, that swarmed upon me from the ancient house. Insufferable and forbidden things besieged me with filthy talons, brushed me with noisome coils, as I tossed through eternal hours and lay staring at the gray square of the storm-darkened window. The dripping of the rain, the sough and moan of the wind, resolved themselves to a dread mutter of half-articulate voices that plotted against my peace and whispered loathfully of nameless secrets in demonian language.

At length, after the seeming lapse of nocturnal centuries, the tempest died away, and I no longer heard the equivocal voices. The window lightened a little in the black wall; and the terrors of my night-long insomnia seemed to withdraw partially, but without bringing the surcease of slumber. I became aware of utter silence; and then, in the silence, of a queer, faint, disquieting sound whose cause and location baffled me for many minutes.

The sound was muffled and far off at times; then it seemed to draw near, as if it were in the next room. I began to identify it as a sort of scratching, such as would be made by the claws of an animal on solid woodwork. Sitting up in bed, and listening attentively, I realized with a fresh start of horror that it came from the direction of the barred chamber. It took on a strange resonance; then it became almost inaudible; and suddenly, for awhile, it ceased. In the interim, I heard a groan, like that of a man in great agony or terror. I could not mistake the source of the groan, which had issued from Sir John Tremoth's room; nor was I doubtful any longer as to the causation of the scratching.

The groan was not repeated; but the damnable clawing sound began again and was continued till daybreak. Then, as if the creature that had caused the noise were wholly nocturnal in its habits, the faint, vibrant rasping ceased and was not resumed. In a state of dull, nightmarish apprehension, drugged with weariness and want of sleep, I had listened to it with intolerably straining ears. With its cessation, in the hueless, livid dawn, I slid into a deep slumber, from which the muffled and amorphous specters of the old Hall were unable to detain me any longer.

I was awakened by a loud knocking on my door — a knocking in which even my sleep-confused senses could recognize the imperative and urgent. It must have been close upon midday; and feeling guilty at having overslept so egregiously, I ran to the door and opened it. The old manservant, Harper, was standing without, and his tremulous, grief-broken manner told me before he spoke that something of dire import had occurred.

"I regret to tell you, Mr. Chaldane," he quavered, "that Sir John is dead. He did not answer my knock as usual; so I made bold to enter his room. He must have died early this morning."

Inexpressibly shocked by his announcement, I recalled the single groan I had heard in the gray beginning of dawn. My host, perhaps, had been dying at that very moment. I recalled, too, the detestable nightmare scratching. Unavoidably, I wondered if the groan had been occasioned by fear as well as by physical pain. Had the strain and suspense of listening to that hideous sound brought on the final paroxysm of Sir John's malady? I could not be sure of the truth; but my brain seethed with awful and ghastly conjectures.

With the futile formalities that one employs on such

occasions, I tried to condole with the aged servant, and offered him such assistance as I could in making the necessary arrangements for the disposition of his master's remains. Since there was no telephone in the house, I volunteered to find a doctor who would examine the body and sign the death certificate. The old man seemed to feel a singular relief and gratitude.

"Thank you, sir," he said fervently. Then, as if in explanation: "I don't want to leave Sir John — I promised him that I'd keep a close watch over his body." He went on to speak of Sir John's desire for cremation. It seemed that the baronet had left explicit directions for the building of a pyre of driftwood on the hill behind the Hall, the burning of his remains on this pyre, and the sowing of his ashes on the fields of the estate. These directions he had enjoined and empowered the servant to carry out as soon after death as possible. No one was to be present at the ceremony, except Harper and the hired pall bearers; and Sir John's nearer relatives — none of whom lived in the vicinity — were not to be informed of his demise till all was over.

I refused Harper's offer to prepare my breakfast, telling him that I could obtain a meal in the neighboring village. There was a strange uneasiness in his manner; and I realized, with thoughts and emotions not to be specified in this narrative, that he was anxious to begin his promised vigil beside Sir John's corpse.

It would be tedious and unnecessary to detail the funereal afternoon that followed. The heavy sea fog had returned; and I seemed to grope my way through a sodden but unreal world as I sought the nearby town. I succeeded in locating a doctor and also in securing several men to build the pyre and act as pall bearers. I was met everywhere with an odd taciturnity, and no one seemed willing to comment on Sir John's death or to speak of the dark legendry that was attached to Tremoth Hall.

Harper, to my amazement, had proposed that the cremation should take place at once. This, however, proved to be impracticable. When all the formalities and arrangements had been completed, the fog turned into a steady, everlasting downpour which rendered impossible the lighting of the pyre; and we were compelled to defer the ceremony. I had promised Harper that I should remain at the Hall till all was done; and so it was that I spent a second night beneath that roof of accurst and abominable secrets.

The darkness came on betimes. After a last visit to the village, in which I procured some sandwiches for Harper and myself in lieu of dinner, I returned to the lonely Hall. I was met by Harper on the stairs, as I ascended to the death-chamber. There was an increased agitation in his manner, as if something had happened to frighten him.

"I wonder if you'd keep me company tonight, Mr. Chaldane," he said. "It's a gruesome watch that I'm asking you to share, and it may be a dangerous one. But Sir John would thank you, I am sure. If you have a weapon of any sort, it will be well to bring it with you."

It was impossible to refuse his request, and I assented at once. I was unarmed; so Harper insisted on equipping me with an antique revolver, of which he himself carried the mate.

"Look here, Harper," I said bluntly, as we followed the hall to Sir John's chamber, "what are you afraid of?"

He flinched visibly at the question and seemed unwilling to answer. Then, after a moment, he appeared to realize that frankness was necessary.

"It's the thing in the barred room," he explained. "You must have heard it, sir. We've had the care of it, Sir

John and I, these eight and twenty years; and we've always feared that it might break out. It never gave us much trouble — as long as we kept it well-fed. But for the last three nights, it has been scratching at the thick oaken wall of Sir John's chamber, which is something it never did before. Sir John thought it knew that he was going to die, and that it wanted to reach his body — being hungry for other food than we had given it. That's why we must guard him closely tonight, Mr. Chaldane. I pray to God that the wall will hold; but the thing keeps on clawing and clawing, like a demon; and I don't like the hollowness of the sound — as if the wall were getting pretty thin."

Appalled by this confirmation of my own most repugnant surmise, I could offer no rejoinder, since all comment would have been futile. With Harper's open avowal, the abnormality took on a darker and more encroaching shadow, a more potent and tyrannic menace. Willingly would I have foregone the promised vigil — but this, of course, it was impossible to do.

The bestial, diabolic scratching, louder and more frantic than before, assailed my ears as we passed the barred room. All too readily, I understood the nameless fear that had impelled the old man to request my company. The sound was inexpressibly alarming and nerve-sapping, with its grim, macabre insistence, its intimation of ghoulish hunger. It became even plainer, with a hideous, tearing vibrancy, when we entered the room of death.

During the whole course of that funereal day, I had refrained from visiting this chamber, since I am lacking in the morbid curiosity which impels many to gaze upon the dead. So it was that I beheld my host for the second and last time. Fully dressed and prepared for the pyre, he lay on the chill white bed whose heavily figured, arraslike curtains had been drawn back. The room was lit by several tall tapers, arranged on a little table in curious brazen candelabras that were greened with antiquity; but the light seemed to afford only a doubtful, dolorous glimmering in the drear spaciousness and mortuary shadows.

Somewhat against my will, I gazed on the dead features, and averted my eyes very hastily. I was prepared for the stony pallor and rigor, but not for the full betrayal of that hideous revulsion, that inhuman terror and horror, which must have corroded the man's heart through infernal years; and which, with almost superhuman control, he had masked from the casual beholder in life. The revelation was too painful, and I could not look at him again. In a sense, it seemed that he was not dead; that he was still listening with agonized attention to the dreadful sounds that might well have served to precipitate the final attack of his malady.

There were several chairs, dating, I think, like the bed itself, from the seventeenth century. Harper and I seated ourselves near the small table and between the deathbed and the paneled wall of blackish wood from which the ceaseless clawing sound appeared to issue. In tacit silence, with drawn and cocked revolvers, we began our ghastly vigil.

As we sat and waited, I was driven to picture the unnamed monstrosity; and formless or half-formed images of charnel nightmare pursued each other in chaotic succession through my mind. An atrocious curiosity, to which I should normally have been a stranger, prompted me to question Harper; but I was restrained by an even more powerful inhibition. On his part, the old man volunteered no information or comment whatever, but watched the wall with fear-bright eyes that did not seem to waver in his palsy-nodding head.

It would be impossible to convey the unnatural tension, the macabre suspense and baleful expectation of the hours that followed. The woodwork must have been of great thickness and hardness, such as would have defied the assaults of any normal creature equipped only with talons or teeth; but in spite of such obvious arguments as these, I thought momentarily to see it crumble inward. The scratching noise went on eternally; and to my febrile fancy, it grew sharper and nearer every instant. At recurrent intervals, I seemed to hear a low, eager, doglike whining, such as a ravenous animal would make when it neared the goal of its burrowing.

Neither of us had spoken of what we should do, in case the monster should attain its objective; but there seemed to be an unvoiced agreement. However, with a superstitiousness of which I should not have believed myself capable, I began to wonder if the monster possessed enough of humanity in its composition to be vulnerable to mere revolver bullets. To what extent would it display the traits of its unknown and fabulous paternity? I tried to convince myself that such questions and wonderings were patently absurd; but was drawn to them again and again, as if by the allurement of some forbidden gulf.

The night wore on, like the flowing of a dark, sluggish stream; and the tall, funeral tapers had burned to within an inch of their verdigris-eaten sockets. It was this circumstance alone that gave me an idea of the passage of time; for I seemed to be drowning in a black eternity, motionless beneath the crawling and seething of blind horrors. I had grown so accustomed to the clawing noise in the woodwork, and the sound had gone on so long, that I deemed its evergrowing sharpness and hollowness a mere hallucination; and so it was that the end of our vigil came without apparent warning.

Suddenly, as I stared at the wall and listened with frozen fixity, I heard a harsh, splintering sound, and saw that a narrow strip had broken loose and was hanging from the panel. Then, before I could collect myself or credit the awful witness of my senses, a large semicircular portion of the wall collapsed in many splinters beneath the impact of some ponderous body.

Mercifully, perhaps, I have never been able to recall with any degree of distinctness the hellish thing that issued from the panel. The visual shock, by its own excess of horror, has almost blotted the details from memory. I have, however, the blurred impression of a huge, whitish, hairless and semi-quadruped body, of canine teeth in a half-human face, and long hyena nails at the end of forelimbs that were both arms and legs. A charnel stench preceded the apparition, like a breath from the den of some carrion-eating animal; and then, with a single nightmare leap, the thing was upon us.

I heard the staccato crack of Harper's revolver, sharp and vengeful in the closed room; but there was only a rusty click from my own weapon. Perhaps the cartridge was too old; any rate, it had misfired. Before I could press the trigger again, I was hurled to the floor with terrific violence, striking my head against the heavy base of the little table. A black curtain, spangled with countless fires, appeared to fall upon me and to blot the room from sight. Then all the fires went out, and there was only darkness.

Again, slowly, I became conscious of flame and shadow; but the flame was bright and flickering, and seemed to grow ever more brilliant. Then my dull, doubtful senses were sharply revived and clarified by the acrid odour of burning cloth. The features of the room returned to vision, and I found that I was lying huddled against the overthrown table, gazing toward the death-bed. The guttering candles had been hurled to the floor.

One of them was eating a slow circle of fire in the carpet beside me; and another, spreading, had ignited the bed curtains, which were flaring swiftly upward to the great canopy. Even as I lay staring, huge, ruddy tatters of the burning fabric fell upon the bed in a dozen places, and the body of Sir John Tremoth was ringed about with starting flames.

I staggered heavily to my feet, dazed and giddy with the fall that had hurled me into oblivion. The room was empty, except for the old manservant, who lay near the door, moaning indistinctly. The door itself stood open, as if someone — or something — had gone out during my period of unconsciousness.

I turned again to the bed, with some instinctive, half-formed intention of trying to extinguish the blaze. The flames were spreading rapidly, were leaping higher, but they were not swift enough to veil from my sickened eyes the hands and features — if one could any longer call them such — of that which had been Sir John Tremoth. Of the last horror that had overtaken him, I must forbear explicit mention; and I would that I could likewise avoid the remembrance. All too tardily had the monster been frightened away by the fire . . .

There is little more to tell. Looking back once more, as I reeled from the smoke-laden room with Harper in my arms, I saw that the bed and its canopy had become a mass of mounting flames. The unhappy baronet had found in his own death-chamber the funeral pyre for which he had longed.

It was nearly dawn when we emerged from the doomed manor-house The rain had ceased, leaving a heaven lined with high and dead-gray clouds. The chill air appeared to revive the aged manservant, and he stood feebly beside me, uttering not a word, as we watched an ever-climbing spire of flame that broke from the somber roof of Tremoth Hall and began to cast a sullen glare on the unkempt hedges.

In the combined light of the fireless dawn and the lurid conflagration, we both saw at our feet the semi-human, monstrous footprints, with their mark of long and canine nails, that had been trodden freshly and deeply in the rain-wet soil. They came from the direction of the manor-house, and ran toward the heath-clad hill that rose behind it.

Still without speaking, we followed the steps. Almost without interruption, they led to the entrance of the ancient family vaults, to the heavy iron door in the hillside that had been closed for a full generation by Sir John Tremoth's order. The door itself swung open, and we saw that its rusty chain and lock had been shattered by a strength that was more than the strength of man or beast. Then, peering within, we saw the clay-touched outline of the unreturning footprints that went downward into mausolean darkness on the stairs.

We were both weaponless, having left our revolvers behind us in the death-chamber; but we did not hesitate long. Harper possessed a liberal supply of matches; and looking about, I found a heavy billet of water-soaked wood, which might serve in lieu of a cudgel. In grim silence, with tacit determination, and forgetful of any danger, we conducted a thorough search of the well-nigh interminable vaults, striking match after match as we went on in the musty shadows.

The traces of ghoulish footsteps grew fainter as we followed them into those black recesses; and we found nothing anywhere but noisome dampness and undisturbed cobwebs and the countless coffins of the dead. The thing that we sought had vanished utterly, as if swallowed up by the subterranean walls.

At last we returned to the entrance. There, as we

stood blinking in the full daylight, with gray and haggard faces, Harper spoke for the first time, saying in his slow, tremulous voice:

"Many years ago — soon after Lady Agatha's death — Sir John and I searched the vaults from end to end; but we could find no trace of the thing we suspected. Now, as then, it is useless to seek. There are mysteries which, God helping, will never be fathomed. We know only that the offspring of the vaults has gone back to the vaults. There may it remain."

Silently, in my shaken heart, I echoed his last words and his wish.

THE MAKER OF GARGOYLES

Among the many gargoyles that frowned or leered from the roof of the new-built cathedral of Vyones, two were preëminent above the rest by virtue of their fine workmanship and their supreme grotesquery. These two had been wrought by the stone-carver Blaise Reynard, a native of Vyones, who had lately returned from a long sojourn in the cities of Provence, and had secured employment on the cathedral when the three years' task of its construction and ornamentation was well-nigh completed. In view of the wonderful artistry shown by Reynard, it was regretted by Ambrosius, the archbishop, that it had not been possible to commit the execution of all the gargoyles to this delicate and accomplished workman; but other people, with less liberal tastes than Ambrosius, were heard to express a different opinion.

This opinion, perhaps, was tinged by the personal dislike that had been generally felt toward Reynard in Vyones even from his boyhood; and which had been revived with some virulence on his return. Whether rightly or unjustly, his very physiognomy had always marked him out for public disfavor: he was inordinately dark, with hair and beard of a preternatural bluish-black, and slanting, ill-matched eyes that gave him a sinister and cunning air. His taciturn and saturnine ways were such as a superstitious people would identify with necromantic knowledge or complicity; and there were those who covertly accused him of being in league with Satan; though the accusations were little more than vague, anonymous rumors, even to the end, through lack of veritable evidence.

However, the people who suspected Reynard of dia-

135

bolic affiliations were wont for awhile to instance the two gargoyles as sufficient proof. No man, they contended, who was so inspired by the Arch-Enemy, could have carven anything so sheerly evil and malignant, could have embodied so consummately in mere stone the living lineaments of the most demoniacal of all the deadly Sins.

The two gargoyles were perched on opposite corners of a high tower of the cathedral. One was a snarling, murderous, cat-headed monster, with retracted lips revealing formidable fangs, and eyes that glared intolerable hatred from beneath ferine brows. This creature had the claws and wings of a griffin, and seemed as if it were poised in readiness to swoop down on the city of Vyones, like a harpy on its prey. Its companion was a horned satyr, with the vans of some great bat such as might roam the nether caverns, with sharp, clenching talons, and a look of Satanically brooding lust, as if it were gloating above the helpless object of its unclean desire. Both figures were complete, even to the hindquarters, and were not mere conventional adjuncts of the roof. One would have expected them to start at any moment from the stone in which they were mortised.

Ambrosius, a lover of art, had been openly delighted with these creations, because of their high technical merit and their verisimilitude as works of sculpture. But others, including many humbler dignitaries of the Church, were more or less scandalized, and said that the workman had informed these figures with the visible likeness of his own vices, to the glory of Belial rather than of God, and had thus perpetrated a sort of blasphemy. Of course, they admitted, a certain amount of grotesquery was requisite in gargoyles; but in this case the allowable bounds had been egregiously overpassed.

However, with the completion of the cathedral, and

in spite of all this adverse criticism, the high-poised gargoyles of Blaise Reynard, like all other details of the
building, were soon taken for granted through mere
everyday familiarity; and eventually they were almost
forgotten. The scandal of opposition died down, and the
stone-carver himself, though the townfolk continued to
eye him askance, was able to secure other work through
the favor of discriminating patrons. He remained in
Vyones; and paid his addresses, albeit without visible
success, to a taverner's daughter, one Nicolette Villom, of
whom, it was said, he had long been enamored in his
own surly and reticent fashion.

But Reynard himself had not forgotten the gargoyles. Often, in passing the superb pile of the cathedral,
he would gaze up at them with a secret satisfaction
whose cause he could hardly have assigned or delimited.
They seemed to retain for him a rare and mystical meaning, to signalize an obscure but pleasurable triumph.

He would have said, if asked for the reason for his
satisfaction, that he was proud of a skilful piece of handi-
work. He would not have said, and perhaps would not
even have known, that in one of the gargoyles he had
imprisoned all his festering rancor, all his answering
spleen and hatred toward the people of Vyones, who had
always hated him; and had set the image of this rancor to
peer venomously down for ever from a lofty place. And
perhaps he would not even have dreamt that in the
second gargoyle he had somehow expressed his own
dour and satyrlike passion for the girl Nicolette — a passion that had brought him back to the detested city of
his youth after years of wandering; a passion singularly
tenacious of one object, and differing in this regard from
the ordinary lusts of a nature so brutal as Reynard's.

Always to the stone-cutter, even more than to those
who had criticized and abhorred his productions, the

gargoyles were alive, they possessed a vitality and a sentiency of their own. And most of all did they seem to live when the summer drew to an end and the autumn rains had gathered upon Vyones. Then, when the full cathedral gutters poured above the streets, one might have thought that the actual spittle of a foul malevolence, the very slaver of an impure lust, had somehow been mingled with the water that ran in rills from the mouths of the gargoyles.

At that time, in the year of our Lord, 1138, Vyones was the principal town of the province of Averoigne. On two sides the great, shadow-haunted forest, a place of equivocal legends, of *loups-garous* and phantoms, approached to the very walls and flung its umbrage upon them at early forenoon and evening. On the other sides there lay cultivated fields, and gentle streams that meandered among willows or poplars, and roads that ran through an open plain to the high chateaux of noble lords and to regions beyond Averoigne.

The town itself was prosperous, and had never shared in the ill-fame of the bordering forest. It had long been sanctified by the presence of two nunneries and a monastery; and now, with the completion of the long-planned cathedral, it was thought that Vyones would have henceforward the additional protection of a more august holiness; that demon and stryge and incubus would keep their distance from its heaven-favored purlieus with a more meticulous caution than before.

Of course, as in all mediaeval towns, there had been occasional instances of alleged sorcery or demoniacal possession; and, once or twice, the perilous temptations of succubi had made their inroads on the pious virtue of Vyones. But this was nothing more than might be expected, in a world where the Devil and his works were always more or less rampant. No one could possibly have anticipated the reign of infernal horrors that was to make hideous the latter months of autumn, following the cathedral's erection.

To make the matter even more inexplicable, and more blasphemously dreadful than it would otherwise have been, the first of these horrors occurred in the neighborhood of the cathedral itself and almost beneath its sheltering shadow.

Two men, a respectable clothier named Guillaume Maspier and an equally reputable cooper, one Gerome Mazzal, were returning to their lodgings in the late hours of a November eve, after imbibing both the red and white wines of the countryside in more than one tavern. According to Maspier, who alone survived to tell the tale, they were passing along a street that skirted the cathedral square, and could see the bulk of the great building against the stars, when a flying monster, black as the soot of Abaddon, had descended upon them from the heavens and assailed Gerome Mazzal, beating him down with its heavily flapping wings and seizing him with its inch-long teeth and talons.

Maspier was unable to describe the creature with minuteness, for he had seen it but dimly and partially in the unlit street; and moreover, the fate of his companion, who had fallen to the cobblestones with the black devil snarling and tearing at his throat, had not induced Maspier to linger in that vicinity. He had betaken himself from the scene with all the celerity of which he was capable, and had stopped only at the house of a priest, many streets away, where he had related his adventure between shudderings and hiccuppings.

Armed with holy water and aspergillus, and accompanied by many of the townspeople carrying torches, staves and halberds, the priest was led by Maspier to the place of the horror; and there they had found the body of

Mazzal, with fearfully mangled face, and throat and bosom lined with bloody lacerations. The demoniac assailant had flown, and it was not seen or encountered again that night; but those who had beheld its work returned aghast to their homes, feeling that a creature of nethermost hell had come to visit the city, and perchance to abide therein.

Consternation was rife on the morrow, when the story became generally known; and rites of exorcism against the invading demon were performed by the clergy in all public places and before thresholds. But the sprinkling of holy water and the mumbling of the stated forms were futile; for the evil spirit was still abroad, and its malignity was proved once more, on the night following the ghastly death of Gerome Mazzal.

This time, it claimed two victims, burghers of high probity and some consequence, on whom it descended in a narrow alley, slaying one of them instantaneously, and dragging down the other from behind as he sought to flee. The shrill cries of the helpless men, and the guttural growling of the demon, were heard by people in the houses along the alley; and some, who were hardy enough to peer from their windows, had seen the departure of the infamous assailant, blotting out the autumn stars with the sable and misshapen foulness of its wings, and hovering in execrable menace above the housetops.

After this, few people would venture abroad at night, unless in case of dire and exigent need; and those who did venture went in armed companies and were all furnished with flambeaux, thinking thus to frighten away the demon, which they adjudged a creature of darkness that would abhor the light and shrink therefrom, through the nature of its kind. But the boldness of this fiend was beyond measure; for it proceeded to attack more than one company of worthy citizens, disregarding the flaring torches that were thrust in its face, or putting them out with the stenchful wind of its wide vans.

Evidently it was a spirit of homicidal hate, for all the people on whom it seized were grievously mangled or torn to numberless shreds by its teeth and talons. Those who saw it, and survived, were wont to describe it variously and with much ambiguity; but all agreed in attributing to it the head of a ferocious animal and the wings of a monstrous bird. Some, the most learned in demonology, were fain to identify it with Modo, the spirit of murder; and others took it for one of the great lieutenants of Satan, perhaps Amaimon or Alastor, gone mad with exasperation at the impregnable supremacy of Christ in the holy city of Vyones.

The terror that soon prevailed, beneath the widening scope of these Satanical incursions and depredations, was beyond all belief — a clotted, seething, devil-ridden gloom of superstitious obsession, not to be hinted at in modern language. Even by daylight, the Gothic wings of nightmare seemed to brood in undeparting oppression above the city; and fear was everywhere, like the foul contagion of some epidemic plague. The inhabitants went their way in prayer and trembling; and the archbishop himself, as well as the subordinate clergy, confessed an inability to cope with the ever-growing horror. An emissary was sent to Rome, to procure water that had been specially sanctified by the Pope. This alone, it was thought, would be efficacious enough to drive away the dreadful visitant.

In the meantime, the horror waxed, and mounted to its culmination. One eve, toward the middle of November, the abbot of the local monastery of Cordeliers, who had gone forth to administer extreme unction to a dying friend, was seized by the black devil just as he approached the threshold of his destination, and was slain in the same atrocious manner as the other victims.

To this doubly infamous deed, a scarce-believable blasphemy was soon added. On the very next night, while the torn body of the abbot lay on a rich catafalque in the cathedral, and masses were being said and tapers burnt, the demon invaded the high nave through the open door, extinguished all the candles with one flap of its sooty wings, and dragged down no less than three of the officiating priests to an unholy death in the darkness.

Every one now felt that a truly formidable assault was being made by the powers of Evil on the Christian probity of Vyones. In the condition of abject terror, of extreme disorder and demoralization that followed upon this new atrocity, there was a deplorable outbreak of human crime, of murder and rapine and thievery, together with covert manifestations of Satanism, and celebrations of the Black Mass attended by many neophytes.

Then, in the midst of all this pandemoniacal fear and confusion, it was rumored that a second devil had been seen in Vyones; that the murderous fiend was accompanied by a spirit of equal deformity and darkness, whose intentions were those of lechery, and which molested none but women. This creature had frightened several dames and demoiselles and maid-servants into a veritable hysteria by peering through their bedroom windows; and had sidled lasciviously, with uncouth mows and grimaces, and grotesque flappings of its bat-shaped wings, toward others who had occasion to fare from house to house across the nocturnal streets.

However, strange to say, there were no authentic instances in which the chastity of any woman had suffered actual harm from this noisome incubus. Many were approached by it, and were terrified immoderately by the hideousness and lustfulness of its demeanor; but no one was ever touched. Even in that time of horror, both spiritual and corporeal, there were those who made a ribald jest of this singular abstention on the part of the demon, and said it was seeking throughout Vyones for some one whom it had not yet found.

The lodgings of Blaise Reynard were separated only by the length of a dark and crooked alley from the tavern kept by Jean Villom, the father of Nicolette. In this tavern, Reynard had been wont to spend his evenings; though his suit was frowned upon by Jean Villom, and had received but scant encouragement from the girl herself. However, because of his well-filled purse and his almost illimitable capacity for wine, Reynard was tolerated. He came early each night, with the falling of darkness, and would sit in silence hour after hour, staring with hot and sullen eyes at Nicolette, and gulping joylessly the potent vintages of Averoigne. Apart from their desire to retain his custom, the people of the tavern were a little afraid of him, on account of his dubious and semi-sorcerous reputation, and also because of his surly temper. They did not wish to antagonize him more than was necessary.

Like everyone else in Vyones, Reynard had felt the suffocating burden of superstitious terror during those nights when the fiendish marauder was hovering above the town and might descend on the luckless wayfarer at any moment, in any locality. Nothing less urgent and imperative than the obsession of his half-bestial longing for Nicolette could have induced him to traverse after dark the length of the winding alley to the tavern door.

The autumn nights had been moonless. Now, on the evening that followed the desecration of the cathedral itself by the murderous devil, a newborn crescent was lowering its fragile, sanguine-colored horn beyond the housetops as Reynard went forth from his lodgings at the accustomed hour. He lost sight of its comforting beam in the high-walled and narrow alley, and shivered with dread as he hastened onward through shadows that were dissipated only by the rare and timid ray from some lofty window. It seemed to him, at each turn and angle, that the gloom was curded by the unclean umbrage of Satanic wings, and might reveal in another instant the gleaming of abhorrent eyes ignited by the everlasting coals of the Pit. When he came forth at the alley's end, he saw with a start of fresh panic that the crescent moon was blotted out by a cloud that had the semblance of uncouthly arched and pointed vans.

He reached the tavern with a sense of supreme relief, for he had begun to feel a distinct intuition that someone or something was following him, unheard and invisible — a presence that seemed to load the dusk with prodigious menace. He entered, and closed the door behind him very quickly, as if he were shutting it in the face of a dread pursuer.

There were few people in the tavern that evening. The girl Nicolette was serving wine to a mercer's assistant, one Raoul Coupain, a personable youth and a newcomer in the neighborhood, and she was laughing with what Reynard considered unseemly gayety at the broad jests and amorous sallies of this Raoul. Jean Villom was discussing in a low voice the latest enormities and was drinking fully as much liquor as his customers.

Glowering with jealousy at the presence of Raoul Coupain, whom he suspected of being a favored rival, Reynard seated himself in silence and stared malignly at the flirtatious couple. No one seemed to have noticed his entrance; for Villom went on talking to his cronies without pause or interruption, and Nicolette and her companion were equally oblivious. To his jealous rage, Reynard soon added the resentment of one who feels that he is being deliberately ignored. He began to pound on the table with his heavy fists, to attract attention.

Villom, who had been sitting all the while his back turned, now called out to Nicolette without even troubling to face around on his stool, telling her to serve Reynard. Giving a backward smile at Coupain, she came slowly and with open reluctance to the stone-carver's table.

She was small and buxom, with reddish-gold hair that curled luxuriantly above the short, delicious oval of her face; and she was gowned in a tight-fitting dress of apple-green that revealed the firm, seductive outlines of her hips and bosom. Her air was disdainful and a little cold, for she did not like Reynard and had taken small pains at any time to conceal her aversion. But to Reynard she was lovelier and more desirable than ever, and he felt a savage impulse to seize her in his arms and carry her bodily away from the tavern before the eyes of Raoul Coupain and her father.

"Bring me a pitcher of La Frenaie," he ordered gruffly, in a voice that betrayed his mingled resentment and desire.

Tossing her head lightly and scornfully, with more glances at Coupain, the girl obeyed. She placed the fierey, blood-dark wine before Reynard without speaking, and then went back to resume her bantering with the mercer's assistant.

Reynard began to drink, and the potent vintage merely served to inflame his smouldering enmity and passion. His eyes became venomous, his curling lips malignant as those of the gargoyles he had carved on the new cathedral. A baleful, primordial anger, like the rage of some morose and thwarted faun, burned within him with its slow red fire; but he strove to repress it, and sat silent and motionless, except for the frequent filling and emptying of his wine-cup.

Raoul Coupain had also consumed a liberal quantity

of wine. As a result, he soon became bolder in his love-making, and strove to kiss the hand of Nicolette, who had now seated herself on the bench beside him. The hand was playfully withheld; and then, after its owner had cuffed Raoul very lightly and briskly, was granted to the claimant in a fashion that struck Reynard as being no less than wanton.

Snarling inarticulately, with a mad impulse to rush forward and slay the successful rival with his bare hands, he started to his feet and stepped toward the playful pair. His movement was noted by one of the men in the far corner, who spoke warningly to Villom. The tavern-keeper arose, lurching a little from his potations, and came warily across the room with his eyes on Reynard, ready to interfere in case of violence.

Reynard paused with momentary irresolution, and then went on, half insane with a mounting hatred for them all. He longed to kill Villom and Coupain, to kill the hateful cronies who sat staring from the corner, and then, above their throttled corpses, to ravage with fierce kisses and vehement caresses the shrinking lips and body of Nicolette.

Seeing the approach of the stone-carver, and know-ing his evil temper and dark jealousy, Coupain also rose to his feet and plucked stealthily beneath his cloak at the hilt of a little dagger which he carried. In the meanwhile, Jean Villom had interposed his burly bulk between the rivals. For the sake of the tavern's good repute, he wished to prevent the possible brawl.

"Back to your table, stone-cutter," he roared belliger-ently at Reynard.

Being unarmed, and seeing himself outnumbered, Reynard paused again, though his anger still simmered within him like the contents of a sorcerer's cauldron. With ruddy points of murderous flame in his hollow, slitted eyes, he glared at the three people before him, and saw beyond them, with instictive rather than conscious awareness, the leaded panes of the tavern window, in whose glass the room was dimly reflected with its glowing tapers, its glimmering tableware, the heads of Coupain and Villom and the girl Nicolette, and his own shadowy face among them.

Strangely, and, it would seem, inconsequntly, he remembered at that moment the dark, ambiguous cloud he had seen across the moon, and the insistent feeling of obscure pursuit while he had traversed the alley.

Then, as he still gazed irresolutely at the group before him, and its vague reflection in the glass beyond, there came a thunderous crash, and the panes of the window with their pictured scene were shattered inward in a score of fragments. Ere the litter of falling glass had reached the tavern floor, a swart and monstrous form flew into the room, with a beating of heavy vans that caused the tapers to flare troublously, and the shadows to dance like a sabbat of misshapen devils. The thing hovered for a moment, and seemed to tower in a great darkness higher than the ceiling above the heads of Reynard and the others as they turned toward it. They saw the malignant burning of its eyes, like coals in the depth of Tartarean pits, and the curling of its hateful lips on the bared teeth that were longer and sharper than serpent-fangs.

Behind it now, another shadowy flying monster came in through the broken window with a loud flapping of its ribbed and pointed wings. There was something lascivious in the very motion of its flight, even as homicidal hatred and malignity were manifest in the flight of the other. Its satyrlike face was twisted in a horrible, never-changing leer, and its lustful eyes were fixed on Nicolette as it hung in air beside the first intruder.

Reynard, as well as the other men, was petrified by a feeling of astonishment and consternation so extreme as almost to preclude terror. Voiceless and motionless, they beheld the demoniac intrusion; and the consternation of Reynard, in particular, was mingled with an element of unspeakable surprise, together with a dreadful recognizance. But the girl Nicolette, with a mad scream of horror, turned and started to flee across the room.

As if her cry had been the one provocation needed, the two demons swooped upon their victims. One, with a ferocious slash of its outstretched claws, tore open the throat of Jean Villom, who fell with a gurgling, blood-choked groan; and then, in the same fashion, it assailed Raoul Coupain. The other, in the meanwhile, had pursued and overtaken the fleeing girl, and had seized her in its bestial forearms, with the ribbed wings enfolding her like a hellish drapery.

The room was filled by a moaning whirlwind, by a chaos of wild cries and tossing, struggling shadows. Reynard heard the guttural snarling of the murderous monster, muffled by the body of Coupain, whom it was tearing with its teeth; and he heard the lubricous laughter of the incubus, above the shrieks of the hysterically frightened girl. Then the grotesquely flaring tapers went out in a gust of swirling air, and Reynard received a violent blow in the darkness — the blow of some rushing object, perhaps of a passing wing, that was hard and heavy as stone. He fell, and became insensible.

Dully and confusedly, with much effort, Reynard struggled back to consciousness. For a brief interim, he could not remember where he was nor what had happened. He was troubled by the painful throbbing of his head, by the humming of agitated voices about him, by the glaring of many lights and the thronging of many faces when he opened his eyes; and above all, by the sense of nameless but grievous calamity and uttermost horror that weighed him down from the first dawning of sentiency.

Memory returned to him, laggard and reluctant; and with it, a full awareness of his surroundings and situation. He was lying on the tavern floor, and his own warm, sticky blood was rilling across his face from the wound on his aching head. The long room was half filled with people of the neighborhood, bearing torches and knives and halberds, who had entered and were peering at the corpses of Villom and Coupain, which lay amid pools of wine-diluted blood and the wreckage of the shattered furniture and tableware.

Nicolette, with her green gown in shreds, and her body crushed by the embraces of the demon, was moaning feebly while women crowded about her with ineffectual cries and questions which she could not even hear or understand. The two cronies of Villom, horribly clawed and mangled, were dead beside their overturned table.

Stupefied with horror, and still dizzy from the blow that had laid him unconscious, Reynard staggered to his feet, and found himself surrounded at once by inquiring faces and voices. Some of the people were a little suspicious of him, since he was the sole survivor in the tavern, and bore an ill repute, but his replies to their questions soon convinced them that the new crime was wholly the work of the same demons that had plagued Vyones in so monstrous a fashion for weeks past.

Reynard, however, was unable to tell them all that he had seen, or to confess the ultimate sources of his fear and stupefaction. The secret of that which he knew was locked in the seething pit of his tortured and devil-ridden soul.

Somehow, he left the ravaged inn, he pushed his way through the gathering crowd with its terror-muted murmurs, and found himself alone on the midnight streets. Heedless of his own possible peril, and scarcely knowing where he went, he wandered through Vyones for many hours; and somewhile in his wanderings, he came to his own workshop. With no assignable reason for the act, he entered, and re-emerged with a heavy hammer, which he carried with him during his subsequent peregrinations. Then, driven by his awful and unremissive torture, he went on till the pale dawn had touched the spires and the housetops with a ghostly glimmering.

By a half-conscious compulsion, his steps had led him to the square before the cathedral. Ignoring the amazed verger, who had just opened the doors, he entered and sought a stairway that wound tortuously upward to the tower on which his own gargoyles were ensconced.

In the chill and livid light of sunless morning, he emerged on the roof; and leaning perilously from the verge, he examined the carven figures. He felt no surprise, only the hideous confirmation of a fear too ghastly to be named, when he saw that the teeth and claws of the malign, cat-headed griffin were stained with darkening blood; and that shreds of apple-green cloth were hanging from the talons of the lustful, bat-winged satyr.

It seemed to Reynard, in the dim ashen light, that a look of unspeakable triumph, of intolerable irony, was imprinted on the face of this latter creature. He stared at it with fearful and agonizing fascination, while impotent rage, abhorrence, and repentance deeper than that of the damned arose within him in a smothering flood. He was hardly aware that he had raised the iron hammer and had struck wildly at the satyr's horned profile, till he heard the sullen, angry clang of impact, and found that he was tottering on the edge of the roof to retain his balance.

The furious blow had merely chipped the features of the gargoyle, and had not wiped away the malignant lust and exultation. Again Reynard raised the heavy hammer.

It fell on empty air; for, even as he struck, the stone-carver felt himself lifted and drawn backward by something that sank into his flesh like many separate knives. He staggered helplessly, his feet slipped, and then he was lying on the granite verge, with his head and shoulders over the dark, deserted street.

Half swooning, and sick with pain, he saw above him the other gargoyle, the claws of whose right foreleg were firmly embedded in his shoulder. They tore deeper, as if with a dreadful clenching. The monster seemed to tower like some fabulous beast above its prey; and he felt himself slipping dizzily across the cathedral gutter, with the gargoyle twisting and turning as if to resume its normal position over the gulf. Its slow, inexorable movement seemed to be part of his vertigo. The very tower was tilting and revolving beneath him in some unnatural nightmare fashion.

Dimly, in a daze of fear and agony, Reynard saw the remorseless tiger-face bending toward him with its horrid teeth laid bare in an eternal rictus of diabolic hate. Somehow, he had retained the hammer. With an instinctive impulse to defend himself, he struck at the gargoyle, whose cruel features seemed to approach him like something seen in the ultimate madness and distortion of delirium.

Even as he struck, the vertiginous turning movement continued, and he felt the talons dragging him outward on empty air. In his cramped, recumbent position, the blow fell short of the hateful face and came down with a dull clangor on the foreleg whose curving talons were fixed in his shoulder like meat-hooks. The clangor ended in a sharp cracking sound; and the leaning gargoyle vanished from Reynard's vision as he fell. He saw nothing more, except the dark mass of the cathedral tower, that seemed to soar away from him and to rush upward unbelievably in the livid, starless heavens to which the belated sun had not yet risen.

It was the archbishop Ambrosius, on his way to early Mass, who found the shattered body of Reynard lying face downward in the square. Ambrosius crossed himself in startled horror at the sight; and then, when he saw the object that was still clinging to Reynard's shoulder, he repeated the gesture with a more than pious promptness.

He bent down to examine the thing. With the infallible memory of a true art-lover, he recognized it at once. Then, through the same clearness of recollection, he saw that the stone foreleg, whose claws were so deeply buried in Reynard's flesh, had somehow undergone a most unnatural alteration. The paw, as he remembered it, should have been slightly bent and relaxed; but now it was stiffly outthrust and elongated, as if, like the paw of a living limb, it had reached for something, or had dragged a heavy burden with its ferine talons.